Romesh Gunes̲ of fiction, inclu Booker-shortlis Books. In 1997 Italy and in 2004 he was elected a Fellow of the Royal Society of Literature. He was born in Sri Lanka and lives in London.

More praise for *Noontide Toll*:

'*Noontide Toll* gives a deceptively gentle, obliquely authoritative and essential tour of post-war Sri Lanka' 'Books of the Year' chosen by Helen Simpson, *TLS*

'Gracefully written ... Humane warmth and bitter irony combine as Gunesekera surveys traumatised survivors, returned exiles, aid workers, shame-stricken army personnel and opportunistic foreign visitors' 'Books of the Year' chosen by Peter Kemp, *Sunday Times*

'Beautiful and haunting ... Not a word is wasted or a detail extraneous in the clenched, explosive vignettes Gunesekera strings together ... [He] is an exceptionally poised and potent craftsman' Pico Iyer, *Wall Street Journal*

'Ever since his early books *Monkfish Moon* and *Reef*, Gunesekera has tended to eschew the jungly, almost choking literary plenitude of his native island. With delicacy, subtlety and sad humour ... [he] cuts away and pares back, to isolate the telling detail, the key image, the life-defining scene' *Independent*

'The narrative is crafted with such care that when the veil of words lifts, the calamity that lurks beneath rises like a tsunami, suddenly real ... beautiful and sad, rising and falling like a love song ... Nuanced [and] beguiling' *Indian Express*

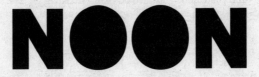

NOON TIDE TOLL

Romesh Gunesekera

GRANTA

Granta Publications, 12 Addison Avenue, London W11 4QR

Published in Great Britain by Granta Books, 2014
This edition published by Granta Books, 2015
First published in India in Hamish Hamilton by Penguin Books India 2014

Copyright © Romesh Gunesekera 2014

The right of Romesh Gunesekera to be identified as the
author of this work has been asserted by him in accordance
with the Copyright, Designs and Patents Act, 1988.

'Mess' was first published in Granta 125;
'Roadkill' was first published in the *New Yorker*

A CIP catalogue record for this book
is available from the British Library.

1 3 5 7 9 10 8 6 4 2

ISBN 978 1 78378 0 174
eISBN 978 1 78378 0 167

Typeset in Bembo Std by Eleven Arts, Delhi
Offset by M Rules
Printed and bound by CPI Group (UK) Ltd, Croydon, CR0 4YY

www.grantabooks.com

MIX
Paper from
responsible sources
FSC® C020471

'There was nowhere to go . . . so keep on rolling
under the stars.'

Jack Kerouac, *On the Road*

Helen

In memory of my mother,
Miriam
1924–2013

Contents

Contents

SOUTH

Full Tank

Every time I drive across the causeway to Jaffna, I feel I am entering another country. The lagoon is as big as a sea. The sky touches it at the edge, on the left, and on the right, and the wind makes the ripples look like waves. The fellows at the checkpoint know me so well now that they don't even look at my ID. They crack a couple of jokes about the state of my van and laugh their heads off. I tell them it is a Japanese van. In 1945, Japan was a dump. Nobody thought the Japanese could make even a cup of tea any more, but now Toyota is the biggest car company in the world. It's a funny business, I tell them. No one knows who will have the last laugh. Look at Germany, same thing. German tourists are rolling in it now. Their chancellor is the boss of Europe. It makes you wonder about this business of defeat and victory.

Today, I am the van man for two Hollanders and Mrs Cooray. I get some oddballs in here, but this is the oddest trio in a while. My job is to drive them to Jaffna for one night only: straight there and straight back. By the end of the trip we would have spent more hours on the road than in the town. Apparently, a guide has been arranged for a morning tour of the place. Some crazy scheme for a renovation project or something.

Mrs Cooray, from the new Heritage Agency, is in charge. 'You have petrol, no?' she asked the moment she got in. She is like the deputy governor's wife I had to chauffeur when I worked at the Coconut Corporation. Before I got my desk job, I used to drive her all around Colombo. It was a good job even though she was another madcap. I preferred being behind a wheel—going somewhere—than behind a desk. That's why I started this business with the van the moment I retired from the corporation. It is a minibus, not a sports car, but it makes me feel young. When I tell my tourists that I retired a year ago, at fifty-five, they are astounded. 'Fucking hell,' Mr Benton from Brighton said. His language surprised me. But that's the way the new breed of tourist talks nowadays, even when they are flip-flopping in their mid-sixties and should know the risks of a loose mouth and all that. They come from such developed countries, but they have to stay in service until they lose their marbles. Then they come here on a tight budget looking for their goolies.

Sometimes I think the way the world is organized is a joke.

The hotel Mrs Cooray booked for the night is off Hospital Street. I have stayed in it before. It is an OK place, but I can't help thinking, we are in a land where every road seems to lead to a hospital. You could say we have all been a little damaged by the last few decades, so I guess that is only right. Up here, in this wounded country, even the sky bleeds every evening.

The Hibiscus Hotel has no star rating. The porch has been repainted in pink but there have been no attempts at improvements inside since my last visit. Even so, our group looks happy enough. I think the Dutch have very low expectations. Maybe because they can't see very far ahead with the dykes and all that. How they ever conquered the world, I don't know. Or even how they set sail on the high seas with their balls of Edam.

Soon it is dark and Kanna, the duty manager, giggles and turns the coloured lights on making the place even more garish. The staff are sweet but there is a long way to go before a hotel like the Hibiscus hits the mark. Jaffna has never been a major tourist destination and is not about to be one—not just yet, whatever the newspapers say.

'We start tomorrow at eight o'clock, Vasantha,' Mrs Cooray says, standing under a glass bowl of fuzzy light. The lampshade is swarming with noisy insects. 'We go to the fort in the morning and after lunch we have a meeting at the Navalar Cultural Hall. You know it?' She searches her handbag for something, then snaps it shut triumphantly. 'Never mind. There will be an army boy here in the morning to show us the way.'

I bow. 'Goodnight, madam.'

She sprays her arms with the small yellow canister she'd found in her bag. 'Goodnight, Vasantha,' she says and floats over to the reception area to join the others, humming the bouncy song she had made me put on, again and again, in the van about a sandman bringing us a dream.

I make my way to the staff quarters. Kanna says I can have the best room to myself this time. Normally, in a place like this, one would have to share but there are no other drivers here tonight. So, I can sleep like a king in a land of dead kings. I ask for a cool beer and Kanna laughs. I tell him I have been on the road for eleven hours and I am very thirsty. He finds the idea of an eleven-hour drive an even bigger joke than a cold Lion lager.

'All that way, just to stay for one night? What do they want?'

'Two of them have come from a lot further. From Holland in Europe.'

Kanna laughs again. 'But not from Hague, no?' He gives me a beer and a plate of roti. I wonder if he gets Channel 4 or Al Jazeera where there has been a lot of talk about the war courts of The Hague. How a small Dutch town like that on the edge of Europe became the conscience of the world is a mystery to me. We could all learn something from that.

Out in the garden, beyond the palmyra, I hear an owl hoot. It has been a long time since I have heard one— an owl. It must mean something, but I am too tired to remember. All I know is that with a van, at least, you are never stuck. You can always get in it and go for a loaf. You don't have to feel trapped. If you are on the move, there is always hope.

NORTH

Folly

When I stepped out in the morning, I found a fellow with a sharp, pointed head examining the wheels of my van. I hadn't seen him at the hotel before.

'Mokadtha?' I asked him, in Sinhala. What's up? Half challenge, half greeting. My smattering of Tamil had already spun out of reach before breakfast. It seemed not to matter to him. Jaffna being what it is today, maybe anything goes.

'This tyre won't last long up here,' he warned. 'You should change it.' A few minutes later, Mrs Cooray and her party appeared under the porch. I pulled open the sliding door of the van with a bit of an effort. 'You need oil,' he added. 'A little squirt.'

Mrs Cooray, dressed in a bright yellow blouse and bountiful blue jeans, came full sail across the courtyard. Her entourage—two Dutch visitors caught in the slipstream—looked crumpled as though they had slept together in a cramped cot.

'Are you Dilshan?' she asked pointy-head.

He blinked. 'Guide, madam.'

'You will take us to the fort?'

'No problem, madam.'

They climbed into the van. The two Dutchmen forced themselves into the narrow back seat while Mrs Cooray, small, round and cheerful, bounced into the spacious middle row. 'Did you rest, Vasantha?' she asked me.

'All right, madam,' I said. I was pleased to see them all back in their places, exactly as they had been for the journey up from Colombo the day before.

Our guide waited until everyone was settled and then jumped in next to me. 'Yamu,' he said, in Sinhala. 'Let's go.'

I started the engine and we rolled to the gate. He gave no other direction, so I turned right on the lane and headed towards the main road. Guides in our country are like that. They don't say anything until you are about to make a wrong turn. Then they shout 'left' or 'right', amazed that you had not divined the correct route. Is it because we are an island people and expect everyone to know the same things like one big happy family? Anyway, I have learnt to go by instinct until I am told not to. What else can you do when everything is so muddled? Happy families are a rare treat. So I turned right again, at the junction, although on this occasion, I have to admit, I did know the way to Jaffna Fort. Our hard-edged guide was there only to get us in through the army security. An off-duty soldier. Moonlighting. Squirting oil, you might say, on troubled waters.

'Did you enjoy your breakfast?' Mrs Cooray asked her two guests, settling herself sideways along the length of the seat.

'It was good,' the taller one, Paul, said, 'but I had hoped they would have some pittu or appam.'

'The hotel just opened a few months ago. They are trying very hard to do proper continentals.'

'The pineapple jam was excellent,' the other man, Vince, piped in.

I hadn't had any people from Holland in my van before. I liked these two. They might have been diplomats, or from some funding agency, but they didn't talk much. On our journey up, I don't think they said more than a couple of dozen words each. But already they have picked up some local terms. Mrs Cooray made up for it though. After coffee in Dambulla, three and a half hours into our journey, she would not stop talking. She gave me a cassette for the player and sang along with the hits of the fifties. In between, we heard everything about her family: from her pickled grandmother in Nugegoda, to her son-of-a-Dalmatian husband who had abandoned her for an Australian horse-breeder even though he couldn't tell a piebald from a jackass. 'What does an Australian jockey have that I don't, huh?' she asked her incredulous guests. I looked in my mirror and saw them exchange looks. 'Two, not one, but two children he fathered,' she said, as though he had been a randy farmer sowing paddy in her field. 'Then he discovers his orientation. Hell of a compass that is, no?' She was now the incredulous one. 'I know in Amsterdam it is all very this and that, but what am I to tell my boys when they grow up? That he liked to go side-saddle in the outback?'

It was not so surprising that the two men kept quiet. 'Left, left.' Our guide thumped the dashboard.

I turned the wheel, unflustered by his sudden fit. In my van, I maintain a sense of serenity, whatever goes on inside or out. People like that. A place of safety. An island of peace. The tips I get are good. They are grateful, no doubt, that I have not killed them, or injured them, or even aged them with squealing brakes and stops and starts. Having paid for a piece of paradise, they are then bombarded with warnings and get worried about travel sickness, dengue, landmines and nerve gas and so are amazed to get to their pleasure pools unharmed. Not only that, they even discover some comfort cruising our colourful roads. In their relief, their generosity gets the better of them. A smooth, safe ride is what I deliver, however long the journey. Not easy on the A9 to Jaffna. Especially after all the rain, never mind the war. Looking at the road, you'd think there'd been an air strike by a bunch of pot-headed monsoon gods. In some places, the craters are bigger than my wheels.

But the ordinary roads in Jaffna are not bad. On a Sunday morning, they are clean and clear. Like down south in the old days. Among the coconut trees and lotus ponds, you hardly notice the bullet-riddled cottages and toppled walls. We got to the fort area in no time. Dilshan jabbed a finger this way and that to get me to go round the cricket stadium to the entrance.

'Look, the sea.' Mrs Cooray beat the back of my seat. The blue bruise in the distance fattened like a mirage and began to sparkle as I took the curve. 'Ten cents for me.'

In my mirror I saw Vince the shorter peer forward. Paul, already stooped inside, turned his head to look out of the side window. 'What's that big white building?'

Mrs Cooray nudged Dilshan. 'Is that the library?' Her voice hit a pitch of disbelief only found in the swankiest shops of Colombo, or on Indian breakfast TV.

'Yes, madam,' Dilshan said. Then broke into Sinhala. 'Eka thamai. That's the one that was burnt in '81. Now completely rebuilt. It looks, they say, just the same.'

'Can we go in?' Paul asked, enthralled.

'No, sir,' Dilshan replied in courteous but firm military English. 'Today not possible.' He urged me to drive on and we sped past the gates and the bronze statue of a Jaffna giant. I wondered how long he had been there, fixed to his strip of scorched earth, pondering the fate of his molested land.

★

The outer walls of the fort form a bare crust that looked to me like the edges of an old wound. I drove slowly to the checkpoint and stopped. The young soldier on guard recognized Dilshan and came up to the window.

'So, how?' Dilshan greeted him. 'Anybody in there today?'

The youngster made a face. 'Nobody comes.'

Dilshan waved his hand as if he was paddling water, urging me to drive on. No further conversation was necessary. Dilshan had credentials bursting out of his biceps. I waited for the young soldier to lift the red pole and then went through. The old stone fort is really a small fortified town with high ramparts, barracks, official residences, the church and so on. Or at least that was what it used to be. Now even the gateway is a ruin.

'Is there any shade to park in?' Mrs Cooray asked. 'The van will get so hot.'

I stopped at the edge of the dried-out moat. 'No, madam. No trees here.' Even the grass had been beaten to dust by the bands of Tiger cadres and the boom pah pah of the Sri Lankan army over the last thirty years.

Dilshan jumped out and yanked open the passenger door. 'Come, madam. We have to walk from here.'

Mrs Cooray peered out suspiciously. 'In this sun? Can't we just drive in a little bit at least?'

'Only army can drive in, madam. This one is a military zone.'

'But you are army, no?'

'Not official duty, madam. Come this way, please.'

Mrs Cooray climbed down and unfurled a polka-dot umbrella. The two Dutch men followed her out. Paul put on a pair of sun goggles that made him bug-eyed, while his companion squinted under a cupped hand. Dilshan led the way doing an occasional parade-ground half-step to keep in line with Mrs Cooray. We headed for the entrance tunnel in military formation, with me bringing up the rear.

'So, this is one of your legacies, Paul, Vince,' Mrs Cooray said loudly. 'It was the envy of the world at one point, you know. Until the troubles came it was a perfectly preserved example of an eighteenth-century Dutch colonial fort.'

'Yes, built in the shape of a star,' Paul said.

'Why did they do that? They didn't have aeroplanes, no? So, who could tell what it looked like? Because that's the thing, no? It is like a star only if you look from above?' Mrs Cooray stopped. 'Was it for aliens?'

'No, no.' Paul lowered his head. 'The fort was built for the eyes of God.'

Mrs Cooray turned to him, nearly smacking Dilshan with her umbrella. 'Wasn't that just the church?'

'No, no,' Paul repeated his newfound litany. 'No. Everything was for God.'

'My goodness,' Mrs Cooray breathed out. 'Everything, huh? For the see-all.'

I looked around. There was a noticeboard on the wall, by the entrance, displaying a diagram and giving a short account of the site as if it were Pompeii and ruined by natural mayhem. The wall itself was crumbling. The tunnel was a mess. It looked godforsaken to me. Mrs Cooray's see-all clearly didn't care eff-all, but I didn't say anything. These days you can't be too careful. Any hole in the country can hide a blabbermouth or a snitch.

Inside the tunnel there were two more soldiers, one at either end. The first one, with a gun hanging off his shoulder, seemed more on duty than the other one who was sitting on a chair and blowing smoke rings. Dilshan saluted and they both straightened up. Mrs Cooray twirled her umbrella. Paul paused to examine some war graffiti.

'Sir, come this way,' Dilshan said.

When we emerged on the other side, we found a large open space the size of a cricket ground. In the centre a few trees struggled to stay awake surrounded by a sea of smashed stones and burnt bricks. The rubble had been organized into sections and the debris sorted according to size and colour. At the far end stood some fragments of bombed-out buildings. The only complete structures were the shrouded military barracks in the far corner.

'There is nothing left,' Mrs Cooray said.

'No, madam.' Dilshan wiped his forehead with the back of his hand. 'Bombs, no. We had many big battles.'

'Battles, here?' Paul leant closer.

'Naturally. Fort, no?' Mrs Cooray pointed at a few pieces of random rubble near a pinkish wall. 'That must have been Kruys Kirk.'

She started walking towards it. We followed. What she hoped to find, I don't know but she moved with an admirable sense of purpose. Her plump heels seemed to swell with every step in the sun.

I know churches get bombed all over the world, from Coventry to Sarajevo, but it was still unsettling to see the results so close up. This was the damage we had done to ourselves like those drunks down by Union Place who smash their faces in the mirror because they don't like the reflection.

Paul touched his friend's arm. 'Look,' he pointed at an egret settling on the ramparts, surrendering to the sea view.

Vince made a low whistle. 'The guidebook says the waterbirds out here are amazing.'

Mrs Cooray turned to him. 'Guidebook? What guidebook?'

'Just something I picked up in Colombo.' Vince pulled out a slim red book from the cargo pocket of his trousers.

Dilshan glanced at the cover and scrunched up his face. His compact skull looked ready to explode. It frightened me like the anger you would see boiling up in the old days. 'What happened here is not written in a book.' He tapped his head with three fingers, the way my father used to do. 'Only in here.'

My father crooked three fingers like that for his gravest warnings. He was only a barefoot caddie at the Royal Colombo, but off the course he was a red-card

Cassandra who kept only the Party manifesto close to his heart. The night our nearby Nazim Stores was attacked by a mob chanting their vile pieties, he drummed his three fingers on his temple in fury. 'The trouble with this country is religion. It puts demons in their heads.' What he would have made of a country at war with itself for three decades, of mad artillery shelling, of armoured divisions and Tiger troops, of air-to-surface missiles and suicide bombers, all the bloody battles of nation and separation, I don't know. Although he rejected religion, he did believe in consequences. It sometimes sounded like dialectical hogwash but, in his view, one thing always followed from another. 'The past,' he would say, 'is unforgiving.'

*

'Madam,' Dilshan said, sharply bringing everyone back to the heat of the moment. 'They say the prison is over there.'

Mrs Cooray seemed to deflate; her mouth puckered by a rush of flattish air. 'What prison?'

'From olden days. Government prison. Judge comes to tea here, bad men go to prison there.'

'You know about the judge?'

'No, madam. Only the prison, and up there, the hanging hole.'

Vince leafed through his guidebook. 'I understand. Yes, that must be the gallows.'

A small cube made of four pillars but no walls stood like a cartoon warning, on the ramparts, visible to all on land and sea. It looked crude enough to have been hatched in a hurry just yesterday.

Mrs Cooray gazed up at it, tilting her polka-dots. Her face was streaming with sweat. 'That's not a hole. Who would they hang up there?'

'Traitors, madam. Have to execute, no? Nowadays we can shoot to execute, but those days they are always using rope.'

'How do you know?'

Dilshan shrugged. 'Have to do it. Orders.'

'You do it? With a rope?'

'No, madam, in war we use the T56. Basic Chinese assault rifle. Very reliable. We go on a mission. We find the target. We execute.' He stared at her, his eyes hard and unblinking. 'Sometimes the target is a woman.'

'You were shooting women?'

'Our enemy had women commanders. Very powerful.'

Vince carefully made a note with his biro. 'Matriarchal system. The warrior mother,' he mumbled. I wondered if he knew about all our queens, prime ministers and presidents. First-timers and old-timers. But before I could say anything, Dilshan turned to him.

'Yes, sir. Even the mother, we have to.' His face stiffened. 'One target we ID'd by her baby. We got notice the K2 area commander was giving milk, so we wait by the hut where the baby was. They try to fool us with ayahs and all, but we know she will be the one who comes and goes and comes again. When I see her slip in like a real kotiya, early one morning, and open her blouse, I knew she is the one. I watch her on a stool, cradling him in her arm, you know. The head just there in the bend of the elbow. I see her lips move, very softly lullabying. She thinks she is safe but I am there. So close, I am hearing her. Same tune, you know, that we have. Tamil words, but same sweet tune we all hear when we come into this world. I wait for her to finish the song and for the baby to have his fill. Let her pat the back and burp him, no? I don't know why but I think it is better if the little one is not left hungry. I watch the sun spread on her face. I see the chain around her throat, with that cyanide capsule of theirs, catch the light.' He twists his hands. 'I have no doubt then what to do, even when she shields the child's eyes and smoothes his head, watching over him as only a mother could.' Dilshan looked down. His eyelids crushed the fluttering memory. 'I don't know if it is right to kill a mother as she is suckling her baby. A hunter will not do that to any animal. You think of your own mother, no?' He paused and started to scratch the palm of his left hand like he wanted to dig something out of it. 'But I wait only for the baby to come off the tit so I can get a clean shot. I made sure I didn't hurt the little one. I waited over my time, no? Maybe that will count for something.'

Without thinking, I said, 'I didn't know they had babies.'

'Why not? They eat and drink and do the same like us. Before a battle the urge is very strong. Man or woman. So, if the war goes on, always you find a lot of babies. Compensation, no? But to us they—mothers, fathers, kids, if they can carry a gun—are first of all, the enemy. That is all. Only now, after it is all done, I feel I am the enemy of myself. I have wounded myself, no? I cannot ever look at my mother again. Never. Not without always seeing that face behind her.' His voice lost its way. The air around us seemed to thicken. Then he added slowly, as though it had never occurred to him before, 'I don't know what that baby will think of us, when he grows up. But I had to do it, no?'

Mrs Cooray pulled out a white hanky and started walking again. Streaks of moisture marked the yellowy folds of her back. Paul caught up with her.

'Interesting fellow, our guide. I had no idea they had to do things like that.'

'It is not like My Lai, or something.' Mrs Cooray

snorted and shook the top of her blouse to let some air in. 'So, what do you think of the fort? Is it a viable project for you?'

'There are possibilities. The heritage dimension is interesting to us but the question is the cut-off point. Architecturally, the Dutch period will be rewarding but expensive. The British period may well be the easiest, especially with the gallows.' He paused. 'The war period, I suppose, is too sensitive?'

'The war is not heritage, Paul. The priority is tourism. What will attract the foreign tourist? We know what the Chinese and Indian tourist wants. Bargains, no? But what about the modern European tourist? They say the beach is not enough these days.'

'Personal stories. That is the best. A pity these soldiers' stories can't be used. You have a living archive, you know.'

'A bigger dead one, I think.' Mrs Cooray patted her face with the hanky. 'I have stories too. My grandfather had many stories about this place. He lived here in the fifties, you know. Apparently the gardens and the tennis courts were all maintained by prisoners. Part of their sentence was this kind of work.'

'The ones not sent to the gallows.' Paul stifled a soft, nasal laugh.

'He never mentioned the gallows. He was a judge here. I don't think it would have been in use in our day.'

'When was capital punishment abolished in this country, Mrs Cooray?'

She looked blank. 'I don't remember.' She pressed a finger to her beaded lip. 'Actually, I don't even know if it ever was. Or whether it got abolished and then came back. Laws come and go, no? That's the thing about Parliament. Everything is changeable. But I haven't heard of any actual death penalty recently. Not even for treason. We had a failed coup in '62. No one was executed for that. Just prison for a while and then they were let out by the Privy Council in London, I think. Anyway, that was already donkey's years ago.'

'But our guide said . . .'

'That is very different, Paul. He was talking about war. A different matter altogether. That is not what *we* are talking about, is it? Not war. That is not a topic for us.' She knew how to shut them up. The small questions that were stirred in my mind quickly evaporated. I could understand her point. You need to check your rear-view mirror, but you can't be looking back all the time—not unless you are in permanent reverse.

Vince who had been scribbling away stopped and closed his notebook. He went over to a section of the rubble cordoned off with white ribbon. He nudged a couple of stones with his foot and then bent down to pick up a fragment of plaster stuck on a brick. 'More graffiti,' he said to the others. 'This is in English.'

'What does it say?' Paul asked.

Vince read out the words slowly. 'Justice of peace.'

'That's not graffiti,' Mrs Cooray said.

'Come and look. It is not an official sign. The words are not complete.'

The egret flapped up from the ramparts. I clutched the keys in my pocket and started to head back to the van, leaving them huddled by the rubble. Dilshan started to say something, but then stopped. Maybe he did know when to keep his mouth shut. My responsibility was only to bring these people to the fort, and take them back without mishap. What they saw, what they heard, what they thought and what they remembered was their problem, not mine. A driver's job is to stay in control behind the wheel and that is all. The past is what you leave as you go. There is nothing more to it.

Mess

In November, I had my first military encounter in Jaffna. Not what you think. Not a skirmish. The war was over. But you could say it was an encounter with the war within: guilt, which I am beginning to see riddles everything. I was asked to take Father Perera and his friend Patrick from England—a younger, balding acolyte—to a military base for a meeting with a big major. Maybe the officer had turned to Christ, in the wilderness, and was looking for the necessary sacrament, or else it was part of the reconciliation effort the bishop was going on about on the radio. At any rate, my mission was to find the camp and deliver the pastors in time for an army dinner. That was fine. I have no problem with our armed forces. They are all heroes now. We have nothing to fear.

A small town about thirty kilometres from Jaffna was our turn-off. At the crossroads by the municipal market, where prawns and pumpkins are bartered and old ammunition shells bought for scrap, a monument commemorated a Sinhala king's first victory over a Tamil prince in the second century BC. It did not seem to point to much of a reconciliation route to me but I took the turn, as I had been told, and tried to pick up some speed. My plan was to do most of the drive before nightfall so that there would be some light to guide me, but my passengers had been too slow getting out of the Hibiscus. I could hear them on the veranda discussing redemption versus education instead of brushing what remaining hair they had on their heads and putting on their evening cassocks, but what could I do?

As we got out of the town, the dark enveloped us. I have heard that in some parts of the world the light of humanity has made a black night impossible—darkness has been dispelled by what *Time* magazine calls 'light pollution'. We could do with some of that pollution here. Especially, if humanity is what causes it. My headlights illuminated nothing. The stars scattered across the sky thinned out. Fortunately, the road was straight.

A whitish crumble fell off the edges but I couldn't tell whether it turned into marshland or salt pans further out.

'Father Perera, did they say how far before the next turn?' The numbers of the milometer tumbled in the glow of the dashboard.

'I was told about half an hour's drive.'

'But at what speed, Father? The army has to march, no? Or they go by tanks. Not Toyotas.'

The acolyte, Mr Patrick, said, 'I have Google Maps on my phone.' Our interior lit up as he switched on his cell.

I slowed down, more out of instinct than practicality. There was no real alternative to carrying on as we were. I heard him tap the screen. I couldn't be sure, but I thought he swore in the bluish glare. 'No signal, sir?'

'The map showed nothing. Just a blank space like a bloody desert and now it's gone off.'

'War zone, sir. Army business, no?'

We carried on mapless in no man's empty sand. After about another fifteen minutes, my headlights picked out a jeep parked by a bumpy white culvert. I made out one soldier leaning against the back, smoking, while another irrigated the desert. I stopped and rolled down the window.

'Is the Samanala Camp on this road?' I asked, in Sinhala.

The smoker came over and peered into the van. 'Why do you want to know?'

I said I was bringing a priest for an important meeting with a big major. 'He is waiting for us,' I said.

The soldier puffed on his cigarette. I thought Father Perera might offer him some guidance on protocol, and that he might take it out of his mouth for a moment, but there was only the tinkle of piss in the dark. Then the soldier barked something at his companion. The other soldier did up his flaps and pulled out his phone. He had a signal but then, of course, he would. How else could an army function? We waited for the talk to subside outside. Then the first one smacked the windscreen and said, 'OK, uncle. Can go.'

The phone boy waved a tainted hand as if he was tossing a grenade. 'Go until you come to a fork in the road. Take the left. One K down you'll come to the camp.'

'How do we recognize it?'

'You will know. There is nothing else.'

★

About ten minutes later, we passed a fence made of barbed wire and brown twigs. Then another soldier stepped out on to the road with a flashlight. He pointed it at a gate. I turned the wheel. It was good to be guided.

I felt deep down I must be a believer like Father Perera. I drove slowly. Long, low buildings disappeared into black. I felt we should be on camels, or at least donkeys. Something more biblical than my van.

'Father, where now?'

'Keep going. There will be a sign.'

A man of faith has much to be thankful for in a world as dark as ours.

Small red border plants flared in neat lines. Clumps of starry flowers blinked. This was a military village with civic pride. An oasis of luxury, rather than a lean fighting unit out of *Spartacus* or *The Guns of Navarone*. The road curved. We came to a lighted building with three magisterial mango trees guarding it. The building had its own inner fence made of dried palmyra fans, more decorative and intricate than anything else around. There was yet another soldier waiting for us. He was the sign. He came forward and opened the side door for my passengers. Father Perera got down first. The soldier clicked his heels. He didn't say anything. Mr Patrick looked ghostly in the lamplight. Father Perera turned to me. 'Vasantha, you must join us.' He sounded like Jesus must have done among the Pharisees, and I began to wonder whether this was how conversion worked. Tonight, I thought, I could be an officer and an apostle. It felt good. I suppose that's the thing about it.

I asked the soldier whether I could park the van around the side. He shrugged. In the military I thought one had to be more decisive and heroic, but perhaps that was further up the chain of command and only in times of real conflict. Peace has made us all dozy, I guess. Even the crickets were muffled.

The room was enormous and had electricity. You could do a wedding party in there, no problem. Red cloths had been laid with crisp folds at the corners. We were ushered to the bar area that had been fitted out with cushioned rattan furniture. The TV in the corner was droning Rupavahini news.

Father Perera took the chair in the centre of the row lined up against the wall; Mr Patrick sat next to him. I went for the smallest corner seat. Outside my van, I never quite know my place. Only that it is very easy to make a fool of oneself in unknown territory.

No one said a word. On TV, Chinese VIPs were shaking hands. Why do people shake hands? Why do the Chinese do it? Did Chairman Mao ever do it? Do any of them wash their hands properly? From what I have seen in comfort stops up and down the country, it is a big surprise who does and who does not wash their hands. Not all foreigners do. Pontius Pilate did, but the Unilever man from Birkenhead, the other day, definitely didn't, despite the discount he must get on soap products. Ordinary soldiers in a desert obviously can't. Or if they are in the middle of a battle or something. That's why hygiene-wise it is always better to keep one's hands to oneself. But perhaps in China they are commanded to wash their hands regularly. Cleanliness is next to godliness, my father used to say. As a Party-wallah, he would have known.

A few minutes later, a small man in white livery limped in carrying a tray with glasses of orange juice and beer and something colourless and sparkling. Father Perera picked a juice, Mr Patrick, a beer. I asked what the other drink was and the man serving cringed as if he thought I might scold him. His skin was flaky. 'Lemonade,' he whispered.

But one needs to know. I have responsibilities. I can't be drinking army gin and tonic and driving back blind as a baboon, whatever the state of the nation.

'So,' Father Perera raised his glass. 'This is very impressive, isn't it?'

'I expected a camp to look more temporary,' Mr Patrick replied. 'Not so solidly built. This is all very settled.'

'Concrete beneath the palmyra.' Father Perera reached behind his seat and slyly prodded the pale-brown leafy wall.

Mr Patrick took out his phone and scrolled through something on the screen. 'A clear shot is all we need,' he muttered. He seemed a long way from ordination.

Then a door opened and a powerfully built man slipped in. His face was proud and full, his smile glittery. 'Good evening, gentlemen. Welcome.'

We all rose to our feet. 'Good evening, Major.' Father Perera's voice shifted up as though he were acting a part.

'Sit down, please, sit down. You have a drink? Good.' The major strode over to the solitary presiding chair under the TV. 'Please sit. Dinner will be served at eight. Is that all right?'

'Very kind of you, Major.' Father Perera sank down first. I followed, falling in line. Mr Patrick stared at our host and fumbled with his chair.

The major's hands, I noticed, were immaculate. Another officer appeared—younger, taller, slower—whose face was round and beautiful, like a woman's, and whose petal-like lips were large and sensitive. 'Captain Vijay, come and sit down.' The major then looked at me.

'Vasantha,' I managed to say. 'My van.' I looked at Father Perera for corroboration but he was too busy exchanging glances with Mr Patrick.

'Good. Welcome, Vasantha. Welcome to the army.' The major turned back to the other two. 'So, you are touring and wanted to see our operation.'

Father Perera took a quick sip of juice. 'Yes, Patrick is in training in the UK. Church, you know, not army, but he was keen to see a real camp. Our mutual friend, Peeky, yours and mine I mean, said you were the man to arrange it.'

'Old Peeky? You went to London with that fellow for one of his Christian conventions, I hear.'

'Actually, a conference on conflict resolution in Berne. Switzerland. He is in tourism, no?'

'Funny bloody business.' The major laughed. 'We were in college together, you know. Then he took the high road and I took the low. Look what happened.'

'You can never tell,' Father Perera assured him.

'I know. The ways of God and all that.' The major put his hands together in a small prayer. 'You should have come for lunch, Father. We could have shown you everything then. But in the dark, what can you see?'

'Yes, quite,' Mr Patrick nodded. His shiny face reddened. He lowered his head as if he had shaved his horns. 'We were hoping to visit one of the IDP camps.'

'That, I am afraid, is not my department. This is only a military camp.' The major cracked his knuckles deliberately, one after another, and made a small fort with his fingers. He was never a man afraid.

No one had mentioned IDP camps while we were in the van. Those pockets in the jungle where

35

hundreds of thousands of Tamil refugees—Internally Displaced Persons—were kept at the end of the war until the government worked out what to do. Or so they say. I had a suspicion that Mr Patrick just wanted to unsettle the major. Perhaps that is how one proselytizes. Internally displace first, then reprieve. The pastor must find a way to go where angels fear to tread, no?

'We have many parishioners back in England who are very concerned about Sri Lanka,' Mr Patrick added, a little nervously. 'I want to tell them what it is really like. We hear such confusing things.'

'That's media, no? It is important for you to see us as we are. After the war, we are now pure administrators, one and all.' The major smiled charmingly and turned to Father Perera. 'Tell me, Padre, you must have been to Jaffna before?'

'I have indeed, but not for a few years.'

'It is certainly time for you to return then. Your flock must be anxious.'

Father Perera bowed. 'Some, but we do have brothers who have been in the area all along.'

'Oh, I know, I know. I wish your brothers had taken your flock out of the war zone and left us a clear field to operate in.' The major demolished the small structure he had made and rubbed his hands together as though he was oiling the joints of a machine. 'So, what do you think? You like our little mess?'

I was taken aback for a moment, until I realized what he meant. Father Perera knew straightaway. 'Very nicely appointed.'

'We've been here for more than ten years. One must do one's best.'

'That is a long time for a camp,' Mr Patrick butted in.

'For us it is home, Patrick. I myself planted the orchard on my first posting.' He laughed like a man used to laughing alone. 'Between battles, you know.'

'The mango trees outside?' Father Perera asked.

'Not those. No, those were here. Pukka trees. You know, the Jaffna mango cannot be beaten. And we have the fruit straight from the tree. When it is ripe, it just falls into our hands. You cannot get a decent mango in Colombo these days, you know. They are all forced to ripen. All sorts of cheap market tricks. None of that here. The real thing you get here. We will have some tonight. You will see.' He spread out his arms. 'I love this country.'

'Sounds like you will not be shifting camp for a while then, after so many years here. You will remain in occupation?' Mr Patrick's face showed thin, craven lines of daily strain more easily than smiles. His was not the face of a regular believer; there was much too much zeal in it.

'Let us not go there, my friend. Politics is not my expertise. I do not try to predict the future. I am a soldier. I do what I am commanded to do.' He flexed his arm and glanced at the captain. 'My job is to keep my men fit, and to keep the peace.'

'I understand. My grandfather was in the army.' Mr Patrick nodded.

'British Army?' the captain asked in surprise, speaking to us for the first time.

'He was at Dunkirk. He stayed on the beach until all his men were rescued. They all were.' Mr Patrick faltered. 'Along with 350,000 other men. All rescued from the beach.'

'350,000?' The major's dark fingers closed in a tight prayer. 'That's a helluva big operation.'

'Boats came from all over Britain. Hundreds of them, from dinghies to battleships. People still talk about it, seventy years on.' The words rushed, crowding out of Mr Patrick's shallow breath. 'It was a big thing. It will never be forgotten.'

A shield seemed to slide over the major's face. 'I know,' he said thoughtfully. 'We had 350,000 to contend with too, in the humanitarian operation after the final fight.'

★

It was a big job, I know, ending the war, shepherding people. We saw the magnitude of the problem on TV. Mr Patrick in England wouldn't know anything about it, but Father Perera would have seen the pictures of people streaming across the lagoon. The victory march. The housing problem. At first, it was difficult to believe. I thought it was all propaganda. My father used to say, even in the old days, the media is an instrument of the capitalist state. He didn't always know what he was talking about, and was blind to the faults of a socialist state, but as a result he has given me a crippling dose of scepticism. So now, I find it hard to believe anything and end up knowing nothing. Never mind the media, I don't even know whether we are living in a capitalist state or a socialist one, a non-aligned one or a crooked one. And when I try to compensate against my prejudices, I end up believing everything and nothing, as if we are living in a country of no consequences.

I am probably exactly the sort of person Father Perera would love to have in his sights. Just ripe and ready to fall, like the major's mangoes, into someone's comforting hands. Clean hands.

*

At eight o'clock exactly the man in white livery struck a small brass gong.

'Come, let us eat.' The major cuffed his subordinate playfully. 'Captain, lead our guests.'

Captain Vijay stood up. 'Please.' He made a soft, gentle gesture with his hand.

Along one side of the room there was a long table with half a dozen clay pots of curries: chicken, brinjal, okra, prawn.

'Where is the stringhopper pilau, then?' The major asked the attendant.

'End dish, sir.'

'You do very well here, Major,' Mr Patrick said, inspecting the table.

'You have to understand what your men need. They need to feel on top. You see, if morale goes, everything goes. Napoleon's secret. That is why he had vinaigrette and champagne, no?' The major's laugh had turned sharper. 'My CO's big joke.'

'Champagne?' Mr Patrick looked around.

'Actually our chief only likes Black Label, but we have first-class supplies. And now, of course, it all comes by road. Before the A9 opened, we had to airfreight everything: chicken, seer fish, tea, everything. Helluva business that was.'

'Between the fighting?'

'That also was a helluva business. People don't like to admit it, but the enemy was no pushover. Very efficiently trained, very passionate and very disciplined. The thing is they were doing it for a very clear purpose. More difficult for our fellows. You can instil discipline and even motivation in a professional army, but that emotional element is a very difficult thing to fire up. You have to go on the offensive until you smell victory. Then you have the aphrodisiac and can go full tilt.'

'I thought they, the other side I mean, were forced to fight.' Mr Patrick took a plate from the stack at the end. 'Families had to give up a child to the Tigers, didn't they?'

'Yes, definitely. But even so, the brainwashing they do very efficiently. We cannot do that, you see. We have to go by the rules.' He pointed at the prawn curry. 'That is a Jaffna special. Very hot. But you must try it. Baptism of fire. That is the way, no, Father?'

'For the soldier, yes, Major. But I prefer to use water myself.'

'But this is Jaffna, Father. Water is in short supply. What we have is firepower.' He laughed again in small, sharp bursts and then cocked an eye at me. 'Come, Vasantha. Eat, eat.'

I helped myself. This was a banquet as good as you'd get at a five-star hotel. We carried our heaped plates dutifully to the table that had been set for us. The two officers took the two ends. I sat next to Father Perera. He shook open a napkin like a white flag. I was not sure what was going on but I guess that's where religion comes in. If you know the rituals, you have no problem.

'This is delicious,' he said. 'You have a talented chef.'

The major beamed. 'An army marches on its stomach.' He patted his own. 'We eat well and take proper exercise. Thirty-six push-ups a minute and a two-point-four-K run every day.'

'I like to run.' Mr Patrick brightened. 'It really frees you up.' The thought seemed to help him get over some of his earlier speech impediments.

The major sized him up. 'Two-point-four K?'

'I like to do about twenty minutes every day. Today, alas, I couldn't, even though I did bring my running shoes.'

'Twenty minutes? That's good. Our run, two-point-four K, we have to do in twelve minutes max. I say, try for ten. You must always have a target, no?' He cocked his hand this time, like a gun, and aimed a finger straight at my head.

I shivered. This was a man who had done it for real, and I don't mean running.

'But you know my real secret for keeping fit?'

Unlikely to be yoga, I thought, but did not utter a word.

'I can't imagine,' Father Perera said. It sounded like the sort of phrase he would use to draw needles out of his flock.

'Badminton. I play badminton every day. War or peace, the shuttlecock is king.'

'Really?' This time even Father Perera did a double take. I guess all three of us saw rocket-propelled grenades studded with feathers shooting through the air.

'My plan is to start a proper tournament here. Not only for my soldiers, but for the civilians as well. Now, wouldn't that be something?' His eyes darted mischievously.

'What do they think of the army?' Mr Patrick asked in a low voice. 'The people here, I mean.'

The major's eyes fastened on him. 'The people are with us now, you know. We have done a lot for them. I don't mean the fighting. In these last few months, my boys have built a dozen houses for the people around here. This is not army policy, you know. They did it in their own time. We used our own money. Hundred thousand rupees per unit. You see, we are on their side. This is our home now. I have lived in the north for fifteen years. Some of my men have lived in Jaffna longer than anywhere else in their lives. They have no other home.' He cracked his fortified knuckles again and I wanted to duck. 'Some even have sweethearts here. Isn't that right, Captain?'

Our dinner was bizarre. My pair of pastors were not doing much converting. I couldn't tell what they were after. Plain curiosity was not Father Perera's thing, even of army courtship practices. And the major seemed like a man who hosted dinner parties in the mess every week instead of polishing off enemies of the state. Perhaps that was what he did as a proper gentleman and an officer. I wanted to ask him, so I did.

I waited for a pause in the conversation and then, while the major was picking his teeth, I went for it. 'Sir, do you get many visitors dining here like this?'

He looked at me in surprise. 'For dinner, hardly ever. People are frightened, Vasantha, to come here in the dark. You have to be a man of true faith, like the good Padre here, to do it.' He dropped the toothpick on the edge of his plate. His teeth gleamed. 'But I believe it is very good for us to interact. It is good for our cook to prepare a meal for visitors. It is good for Captain Vijay here to meet people. Otherwise, he never wants to go outside, no? I feel very strongly we must prepare our boys for civilian life, to mingle with ordinary people, with tourists. It is not easy, as I'm sure Father Perera can tell you, to break the habits of war. It is a very rough and bloody business. But, you see, they can't be heroes for ever. We have to do the TLC, no? Tender loving care.'

The captain placed his knife and fork together, looking forlorn.

'And you, Major? Are you here always as well?' Father Perera asked. 'No gallivanting?'

'We all stay cooped in too much, Padre. That is our trouble. You see, in the army we all know what to do. Discipline, routine, keeps us on the straight and narrow. Whoever the enemy, we do not fear. A command line is a great source of comfort, no? But when I visit my family, I am in a jungle. Last month I had to go to my daughter's new school in Negombo to see the headmistress. A small matter about music examinations. But, I tell you, after ten minutes waiting for the madam outside her office, I was shaking. You could hear her in the next room. A formidable voice. Used to be at a convent in Panadura, they say. I have never been so frightened in any battleground. With a woman like that, what can you do?' He waved his whole arm in the air. 'She'd drive a fellow bonkers.'

For a moment, I saw him spraying the school office with a machine gun. Lobbing a shuttlecock on to her lap. Going bonkers!

The man in white shuffled around, clearing the table.

'Mangoes,' the major said. 'Now you will taste the best mango in the country. No longer the forbidden fruit, eh?'

Father Perera smiled.

The fruit came cut in segments with the seed separated from the cheeks. The major was right. It tasted like honey on a spoon. I slowly savoured it while Mr Patrick prattled on about harriers and barriers. Their conversation was like a low-key gun battle: each taking potshots in turn, hitting nothing but exchanging fire. Father Perera retreated and, like me, concentrated on his mango. He was quite an expert at scooping every shred of flesh off each slice. Would he suck the seed? He did. I followed suit.

When we were done, coffee was served. Our Major TLC leant forward with his elbows on the table. 'So, Padre, you see, we are not such beasts, are we? We just do the best we can in difficult circumstances, like everybody else.'

*

Our goodbyes were brief. But before I went for the van, Mr Patrick said he would like a photo with the major and Father Perera. He asked me to take it and handed me his phone. Smart Japanese job with face detection built in, but I had to ask them to cosy up to get all three in the frame. The major was in the middle but the other two seemed to veer away however much I asked them to lean in. Mr Patrick had a funny look but I took a couple of OK shots. While he checked the photos, the major said to Captain Vijay, 'Now you take one with Vasantha and me.' He handed him a squatter, meaner bit of kit. I went and stood next to the major. He put his arm around me and squeezed my shoulder. His fingers were strong enough to crush my bones. I could hardly breathe. I thought my chest would burst.

Afterwards, the major called for a bag of mangoes. 'Vasantha, you take those. Best mangoes in the country. Give them to your family as a souvenir from Jaffna.'

Safely back in the van, I turned off the interior light and started heading back towards the gate. The soldier with the flashlight waved us off. It didn't seem right to say I had no family to the major. I have a van, nothing else. For some reason, I was too frightened to tell him the truth. It is a problem a lot of us seem to have these days.

On the road, I kept to a steady fifty kilometres per hour. It was a straight road and there was nothing to worry about, but I didn't want to go fast. We all needed to catch up with ourselves.

Father Perera was the first to break the silence. 'You changed your mind?'

In my mirror, I saw Mr Patrick tap his phone. 'No, I think he is the man. Look, this was the picture we had. The one she took.'

Father Perera squinted. 'Everything is blurry. You can't really be sure of the face.'

'I am sure. He admitted he does go to Negombo.'

'That's his home town. He is a college man. Educated, no? I even know his alma mater there.'

'So? Education is not inoculation. Pol Pot studied in Paris. I can assure you, Marion has been very thorough. She zeroed in on just two possibilities and we know the other guy is dead.'

'But all she had to go on was the girl once saying that she was seeing a senior officer from the north. What if she meant a Tiger commander?'

'That's impossible, Father. You know that.'

I stepped on the accelerator and moved up to forty. A wild cat, or something, bounded off the road ahead.

These trips I do up north are never the same. Each time I find something new about what has happened to our country, and to us. I had never met an army commander before although there are hundreds now, all over the place. The ones on TV are always solemn, with thick moustaches, or barking mad. This major had no facial hair. He spoke like a company man on an executive escalator. Full of himself, true, but that, I have noticed, is one of the characteristics of a confident achiever. I used to see a lot of them in my last job. City folk on a fast track. Now I tend to see only people who are on holiday or on their trip-of-a-lifetime or, like Father Perera, on soul-rectifying missions. Business that requires a much slower pace. Fifty kilometres per hour is ample. But a fighting man, I can see now, has to be one step ahead always and learn to cover his tracks, if he is to survive.

'So, if he is the one, what next?' Father Perera asked.

'I have to talk to Marion. She is the one who knows the girl's family. He has to be brought to account but it will be a painful process for all of them.'

'What about the military?'

'This country is not ruled by the military, is it? He beat her up and left her to die. If he can do that in his home town, imagine what he would have been like in a war zone. They will wash their hands of him.' Mr Patrick jabbed hard at the cushion next to him. 'He is a fucking murderer. Surely he must be punished?'

'I am not a judge, I am only a priest.'

'I am neither, but I know what is right and what is wrong. I told Marion, if anyone could get us to this psycho, you could, Father. And I was damn right.'

'I got you to this major, that's all. I don't know what he is.'

The words hung in the back of the van like smoke. Why is it, I wondered, that some of us cannot shake our doubts whatever we do while others can be so dead sure of things? All I have for certain is a weird sense of complicity and the more I try to escape from it, the more it seems to grow. I wanted to ask the Padre, why is that? He should know but it was not my place to ask questions any more. I was only the driver now, no longer a fellow diner. They were deep in their own matters—talk that didn't make sense to me. The major had been decent enough. Mr Patrick was the one proving to be dodgy.

The town, when we reached it, was quiet. A corner shop had a light on, a white fluorescent flare. One eating place was still open. Nothing else. I stopped at the junction and waited for a man on crutches to cross the road. I remembered how when we were coming I noticed several people with missing limbs in this town. There was a lot of damage around that one gets accustomed to very quickly. The burst shells of houses around Kilinochchi, which I have passed a dozen times or more; the wasted fields. The first time you see a toppled water tower or a building with its sides ripped off, it is undeniably a shock. This was the war, you think. But then soon after that a pile of debris, a flattened home or a broken man just becomes the surroundings. It is simply what is there. What happens. Like a soldier whacking a shuttlecock or a padre sucking a mango. You don't look twice. You don't think about the boy who lost his home to a whistling bomb, or his mother who stepped on a landmine and lost both feet and now has to hobble around on stumps. North or south, you try to avoid thinking too much. What to do? You put a cassette in the machine and sing along to a song about moonlight and love. Paddy fields and doves. It is normal, you say. We have to live in a normal world, whatever happens. Is that wrong?

The major did not seem to me a bad man. He was very correct in his manners and acknowledged me in a way that many people in the civilian world don't. Not just with the mangoes, which was a treat, but in talking to me. No one has asked to have their photo taken with me before, except tipsy foreign tourists. No doubt he could kill a man without batting an eyelid, but I could not believe he would have really beaten a woman to pulp while visiting his family. How could he? I waited for Mr Patrick to say something more incriminating.

His phone beeped. 'I'll text Marion and say we found him,' he said.

Father Perera shook his head. 'We only have a fuzzy little picture that looks a bit like him, Patrick. No real evidence that he even met her. You should have asked him. Confronted him. If he is guilty, there would have been a sign.'

Mr Patrick was sweating even though the air con was on full. His face blazed. 'Do you really have any doubt? Did you not see his hands? When we post the picture the driver took this evening, I am sure someone will recognize him. The two of them must have been seen together somewhere.'

'I don't know, Patrick. I just don't know.'

To my mind, Father Perera was not giving Mr Patrick much pastoral guidance. The kind we need in times of trouble. I was also not too happy getting dragged in as the picture taker. Matters are a lot clearer to a military man. They are trained to make quick decisions and fast exits. Although in Jaffna, I have to say, the major seemed to be in no hurry to leave. But then, if he is the monster they say he is, where can he go? Where can a big man who loses it go? After all, people do lose control, don't they, in times of war? The whole business is insane anyway, killing and maiming like there is no tomorrow. How can you shoot someone in the head and call it duty? How can anyone be normal after that? Father Perera was right. They should have asked him, not assumed. Got him to talk more about himself than their crazy PE routine and the taste of forbidden fruit. Father Perera should know how it works. That's his field, after all. Redeeming the sinner, rectifying our faults. Drawing confessions. I believe Christians say there is nothing that cannot be absolved, if admitted. I'd like to ask him if that is true. It would make a difference, not only for the major but for all of us.

Deadhouse

D r Ponnampalam was in a short-sleeve safari jacket of the sort I have not seen in a dozen years, but he was well turned out, unlike his son—a scruff from the tips of his uncombed hair to the tangled mess of his trainers. The boy must have been in his late teens and looked like he had not seen daylight before noon for years. He yawned. 'No latte, no nothing. What a dump.'

'That was good island coffee, Mahen.' Dr Ponnampalam's head, a small ball perched necklessly on the larger ball of his body, dipped.

'Not even Nescafé. Half a teaspoon of rubbish in a pot like a watering can.'

The doctor ignored his son's grumble and greeted me. 'Good morning, Vasantha. You slept well, I hope.'

'Thank you, doctor,' I said. 'They give us tour drivers from Colombo good rooms here.'

The boy scrunched up his face into as different a shape as he could from his father's. 'Upstairs, no air con. No nothing.'

His father glanced at the road. 'Did you ask how to get to the place, Vasantha? I don't recognize *any* of this.' He spread his hands as he must have done to carry his baby son once, before the boy turned into something he could not understand, like this land. If I had been a father, I would have made sure my son knew our proper place in the world. It is good to know where you stand. But maybe that is not so easy if you are uprooted like these two.

I pulled out a piece of paper that the receptionist, a much smilier young man than the doctor's son, had given me. An eagerly drawn simple map, A to B. 'Only ten minutes in the van,' I said. 'Past the hospital.'

'You can find the hospital?' His face relaxed at the thought of familiar ground. 'Then we are OK.'

Mahen, the boy, got in and sat right at the back where I have the windows screened with batik curtains—a special recent touch for the new sun-avoiding visitors we attract: Gulfers, gangsters, pilgrims of pain. Our peace dividend. He stretched out, ready to sleep. His father placed himself in the middle of the middle row from where he could see in every direction, unimpeded. On our way up, he had told me that this was his first visit back to Jaffna since his boyhood. He went to England as soon as he got the chance in 1952 and never wanted to come back. 'Was England so good those days?' I asked. It doesn't look very inviting now from what you see on BBC World. He said it was very hard going, but he was young then and wanted to make something of his life. He said this partly for the benefit of his son, I think, but the boy pretended to doze. 'And you did well, sir,' I said. The boy's eyelids flickered. 'You became a doctor and now you can come back and do something,' I added a little louder to stir the boy. This country needs doctors. 'I am not a medical man,' he explained, settling down. 'I am a student of history. Now that the war is over I am coming back to see what is left of the nightmare.' He said he was not sure what he would find, and whether he really wanted to see the place again but he felt he had to come back and look for his own history. He was not the only one. I see a lot of them these days. People looking for something long lost and irretrievable like childhood—their own, or their children's. Sometimes

I feel I am also a kind of doctor and that the journey I help them with is a form of healing. With these two, it was night by the time we crossed the border on our way up. We arrived in darkness and they saw nothing until we turned into the lighted porch of the Hibiscus. I think Dr Ponnampalam was relieved. 'I need time to adjust. After all this time, I still need a little more time.'

I turned off Hospital Street and headed towards the ponds. I knew this area from my last trip. We passed the bright white GTZ house, the German NGO base where Mrs Klein stayed when she was up here, and took the shady lane marked by a cross on my map. I think the cross signified a sentry point. There certainly was a small green hut at the spot, crumpled with sandbags; a couple of soldiers in there looked as lost as the rest of us. In my mirror I could see the doctor tighten up. He was not, I think, by nature a tense man but guns, even if they are not pointing at you, can have that effect. You don't have to be Tamil to feel anxious.

'Soldiers everywhere, but nothing to do,' I said to comfort him. 'They only smoke now.'

He was not convinced and looked around nervously for the fire that he was sure was burning, or some other sign of malice.

I took another turn. On this road the houses were bigger. We passed a guest house that looked a cut above our small hotel. Although several of the houses by the road were squat mid-century buildings squeezed into subdivided front gardens, there were older villas visible behind them. I asked the doctor whether he recognized the road.

He peered out. 'This is the one?'

'It's the road the man said to go to. More houses now, but the road is the same. Not widened.' I know when a road has been widened. It doesn't have wiggly bits like this. Our road makers, north or south, are lazy buggers and like to bulldoze everything. Straighten things out in their sleep. 'Can you imagine it without these new houses?' I asked. It was his road after all, not mine, whatever they say on TV about Jaffna belonging to us all. He is the one who lived here as a child, not me.

'I can't. I remember coconut trees, a breadfruit tree in the garden. This is not it.'

Mahen pulled back one of the curtains. 'Stop,' he yelled.

We were going slowly, so I could stop the van without mayhem.

'Reverse. Go back.'

'What did you see?' his father asked.

I checked the mirrors and reversed until the boy again said, 'Stop.'

'Look.' He pointed at a skinny, brown dog sniffing around a small opening in a mass of overgrown foliage. Behind the broken gate I could see the remains of a small Catholic shrine. 'Didn't you say there was some churchy thing on your road?'

Dr Ponnampalam stared at the garbled structure, rebuilding it chip by chip in his eyes. 'Yes, son. Well done,' he said at last. 'That could be it. There were a lot of flowers in there. I used to catch butterflies at the back.'

'House is nearby then?' I asked.

'Past that bend. On the other side of the road. Let's go, driver, let's go.'

After nearly sixty years of staying away, suddenly he was in a big hurry as though it might disappear before we got there.

*

Dr Ponnampalam must come from a very well-to-do family. That is how he could go to England and become a doctor without medicine, while people like us go up and down the same old roads hoping for nothing more than a change of hoardings. This house, his family home, was enormous. It rose like a giant beast through the tangle of overgrown ferns and bushes and trees. We could only see a part of its elephant-like side. It had been built at a peculiar angle. Not facing the road, as though it disdained public thoroughfares and had its own kingdom to rule.

'Palm Villa,' the doctor sighed. There was a blackened sign nailed to the limy wall that confirmed he was right, and half a dozen coconut trees sprawled around the front garden proved the point in a lackadaisical sort of way.

'Your house, sir?' I asked. His son must surely be impressed, I thought. I wanted him to be moved. Despite our differences in class, wealth and race, I could see something of myself in each of them and I wanted the elements to meet.

Mahen whistled. 'Massive.'

The metal gate of spiralling ironwork had a thick chain wound around it secured by a fat padlock. I rattled the gate while father and son got out and stood a little closer together than before. Closer than I had ever done with my father.

'I never really believed I would ever see it again,' the doctor said softly.

'But that's why we came. You've been planning this ever since you retired.'

'Ten years ago, there was a chance with my VER. Voluntary early retirement.' He said the words like a prayer and looked up at the sky. 'But we missed it because of your mother's illness. Then it got bad again. By 2009, the war was intensifying. You remember all those reports?

BBC? Channel 4? How could I think of coming back? I couldn't even imagine it. It was only after Olwyn came six months ago that I thought I must. If he can come, why the heck can't I?'

I heard a sound from the house. A door opened and a man crossed the veranda and disappeared down the steps at the front of the house.

'Someone is there,' I said to the others.

About a minute later, the bushes parted and a young man in jeans and a striped polo shirt appeared—his hair gelled up and his eyes puffy as though he too, like the youth of today, had only just woken up.

We all waited. Lost for words, if not language itself. But as I was only the driver, not the leader or even the guide, I bided my time. Eventually, Dr Ponnampalam broke.

'Vanakkam,' he said hesitantly in Tamil and then reverted to English. 'Who lives here?' Despite his many years abroad, he could tell the young man was a minion.

'Only me, sir.'

'Who are you?'

'Milton, sir. Manager.'

'This was my house.'

'Sir?'

'I used to live here.'

'With madam?' The puffy eyes widened. 'She is coming. She will be here eleven o'clock. Madam Sujitha.'

Mahen took up his father's cue with an exuberance I had not suspected. 'Who the fuck is Madam Sujitha?'

'Son,' his father tried to stem the language and yet spur the unexpected vigour of his progeny. 'Please.'

'This is her guest house. She lives next road and will be coming soon.'

I thought I could get Mahen engaged a bit more. 'Maybe you can look inside then?' I suggested.

'Yeah, can we?'

Milton scratched his head. 'Look? Can do.' He searched his pockets and found a key. With some difficulty, he managed to open the padlock and undo the chain. The gate had to be lifted up an inch to swing open as the hinges had bent and made the corner dig into the ground. It was not designed to encourage guests. He lowered the gate back into position behind us and then led the way to the house. We scrambled through a jungle to get to the front where once upon a time, I imagined, the young Dr Ponnampalam in his short trousers would have been greeted by manicured blossoms and a sparkling veranda. Instead, we came to an enormous, bony tree that cast a gloom over the crumbling building. Close up, you could see that the wood everywhere had warped, the pillars had gone wonky. It looked like a large, dishevelled, shabby drunk barely able to stand rather than the majestic thing we had glimpsed from the road.

Dr Ponnampalam leant back, trying to take the full measure of the old house in one gulp.

'You like to see the bedrooms, sir?' Milton seemed to have perked up. I don't think he had much practice in the business. I asked him how many guests were staying. The sandwich board propped up against the wall seemed unlikely to catch many passers-by.

'Zero. Right now, no one staying. We are making the rooms ready.'

'Not yet open then?'

'We are open. But no guests, no. Not yet. Madam says that someone is coming soon, so we have one room ready. Almost. Come to see.'

I noticed a desk at one end of the veranda. Another uneven sign on it—THE MANAGER—in dull white block letters with an open copy of *Hi!!* magazine providing the only gloss. The front room, the foyer you could say, was empty except for the stairs.

Milton waved us on. 'Upstairs.'

In unfamiliar territory, one should be cautious. After thirty years of war, you learn that. I tested each wooden step before putting my full weight on it, but the doctor seemed to have slipped into a reverie. He climbed up with his head rolling from side to side as if the gentle rocking would reconcile the sad dust and disrepair around us to the cherished images of his childhood. At the top,

Milton led us out on to the balcony. The large tangled garden spread out below us, one part of it sunken like a wreck. The bushes and trees seemed to tumble into it in splashes of red and green.

'Bedroom number one round the corner,' Milton said. 'But please be very careful.' He pointed out a gaping hole in the floorboards. 'Damage to be repaired tomorrow.'

He went ahead to the end of the balcony and pulled open a curtain. We all trooped into the large room. In the centre stood a sturdy wooden bed with bright spindles at the head and foot and a four-inch foam mattress that looked as hard as a squashed loaf of stale country bread. A new mosquito net was bundled up and hung from a rope hooked to an impressively high ceiling of the kind required by the high-born, be they English, Tamil or Sinhala. Near the window there was another smaller bed with a metal frame that might have belonged in a hospital.

'No door?' I asked.

Milton shrugged. 'Every day power cut. So no AC. Anyway no need to hide now.'

'Where was your room?' Mahen asked his father. 'Was it this?'

Dr Ponnampalam looked distraught. 'I don't remember this room. This is very big. Everything is bigger. I thought it would be smaller.'

'Was it up here? Could have been, no?' I asked, as keen as everyone to find a home for what they call the diaspora.

'Yes, but not here.'

'Back room?' Milton asked. 'Very nice back room with a view of the church?'

'I remember I could see the church.' The doctor's eyes dilated as he slowly turned around.

We shuffled into the centre of the house and Milton showed us the other room. There were boxes and pieces of wood, a trestle table with a saw and a hammer on it. Milton said it was the workshop. The carpenter was coming tomorrow. The doctor went in. There wasn't room for all of us, so I stayed out.

'I don't see the church,' Dr Ponnampalam cried, disappointed.

'Sorry, sir. Used to be able to see, before the bomb.'

I don't understand what people like Dr Ponnampalam want from life. Don't get me wrong. It is not a Tamil–Sinhala thing, but the richer you are, it seems the more muddled you get. What would make a boy growing up in a house like this want to leave? He left long before the Tigers could even miaow, years before their great leader took his first potshot. Now the big shot was dead with a hole in his head and the blood of thousands has soaked the land, while Dr Ponnampalam has a balding head and a hole in his heart which he can't seem to fill for love or money. But a big house, I suppose, is not always a happy house.

There was a beep of a car horn from the road. Milton hurried down the stairs.

I went out on to the balcony to look. The gate creaked and a few minutes later a lady appeared by the front steps with Milton. She had her grey hair tied in a bun and was dressed in sporty clothes like a Galle Face jogger on a suicide mission.

From below me, Dr Ponnampalam emerged.

'So, what do you think of it?' she asked. 'We are updating everything.'

'It's not how I remember it.'

'Ha. Nothing ever is. You will have some Nescafé?'

I heard Mahen hiss, '*Yes*.'

She turned to Milton. 'Bring the coffee, and that tin of biscuits.'

I could do with some coffee too, if it was on offer. I made my way downstairs.

Madam Sujitha was standing with a hand on her hip, a woman of scary authority. 'So, Milton says you lived in this house?' she asked the doctor.

'As a boy. Sixty years ago. I was just looking at my room.'

'My father never liked this house. He used to say that it was a millstone around our family's neck. He rented it out but it never paid, he said. Perhaps it was better for your father than mine.' I think she was trying to build a bridge, but I wouldn't want to be anywhere near it if she was planning to blow one up.

'I liked it, but at night I used to get very frightened. There were all sorts of noises. I thought it was haunted.'

'So, you are looking for the ghost now?' She laced her fingers over her face and peered as if through a balaclava.

Milton came with a coffee jar and put it on the desk. Another young boy brought some small cups and a pot of hot water.

Madam Sujitha said that she never knew the house or its occupants when she was young. After she got married she went to Canada. 'We didn't want to stay. It was a bad time. The 1980s.' She laughed. 'It has been bad times ever since I was born, my father claimed. He was right. He was shot on those steps.' She spooned out the coffee in small measures. 'He wouldn't stand for any nonsense. He spoke his mind, you see. He'd make a fine ghost to frighten little boys.'

'Oh my God, I am sorry.' Dr Ponnampalam seemed oddly shocked by death.

'Why are you sorry? You were not one of the assassins, were you?'

'Was it LTTE or army?'

'Why? Who did you give your money to?

'I live in England. I left before you were born.' He lowered his head.

Milton handed out the cups. No milk, no sugar.

'So, no little diaspora donations to our Tigers? No investments in government bonds to fight them? No hedging your bets?'

From the increasing anger in her voice, I wondered for a moment whether she had killed someone herself. She, like me, belonged to a generation that had gone mad enough for anything to be possible. But then something in her face subsided. 'Never mind all that. You are here to make peace with the past for your son, no? Come, sit down. You must sit in your old house after coming all this way.'

She led the way down the veranda to where a few cane chairs lay like smaller shipwrecks pulled ashore. She took the straightest chair while Mahen sprawled on the only cushioned one. The coffee seemed to have extinguished the spark he had shown when we first entered the house, or perhaps it was the numbing effect of talk about the past. His father seemed wary, having learnt recently the need to test everything first. He gently moved one of the chairs a few inches before sitting on it.

'So, you came back from Canada? After the war ended?' he started tentatively.

'Ended?' she laughed. 'No. No. I came back twenty years ago. In Canada, at our central library, I went to a talk and I was awakened. Politically, you know. I was young and idealistic. I had to come back and do what I could for our country. There was a lot to do.' She turned a hand in the air as if to spin a top towards Mahen. 'There *is* a lot to do.'

Which country? I wondered. Whose side was she on? The diaspora, we have been told, are the troublemakers and if it was she rather than Dr Ponnampalam that they meant, I could well understand the headache.

'You came home,' Mahen said softly with a note of admiration that worried me. But I was pleased he had been listening. Tomorrow belongs to youngsters like him but what could he do with it if he didn't know anything about yesterday?

I looked at the rampaging bushes, the twisted trees, the broken wall. You don't need a tsunami to wreak havoc.

'We had three houses. They were all empty. I was the only person in the family left. I started a school in one, kindergarten. Montessori. You know. Something like that, but my own style, you know. And we lived in the other. A small house. Not haunted like this one.' She laughed again. 'No, this was in a really bad state. I don't know when your family left, but it was very broken down. Wild animals only. I think everyone was frightened of this house. Maybe like you they also thought it was haunted. Luckily.'

To my mind it was more a gloomy house, depressed like an old man at the end of an unfulfilled life, rather than a bad place. Benevolent even, despite the mess it found itself in. It was she they would have feared. But then I grew up in a shack next to a cemetery in Colombo. I have no problem with ghosts. These days, in this country, no one can afford to worry about ghosts.

'Why is that?' the doctor asked, inclining his head, more like a student than a doctor. 'Why luckily?'

She leant forward and spoke so urgently that I assumed she was describing events from last year at the end of the war. But the central events were to do with the LTTE retreat from Jaffna in the mid-nineties. 'I was living in our main house, near the school, when the LTTE order came to evacuate. Government forces were gaining ground, you remember? LTTE strategy has always been to draw back into the jungle when threatened, leaving nothing for the occupiers. No population. They may have invested in gold in Bangkok and Singapore, but here they always knew people were the only real asset. Half a million people left Jaffna in twenty-four hours. The whole place became a ghost town, not just this house of yours, doctor. All of Jaffna became a ghost town.'

Mahen had been roused by the urgency of her

voice and was leaning forward. I didn't want her to stop, whatever her politics were. As Dr Ponnampalam was mesmerized, I butted in. 'So, you left? That was lucky?'

She laughed. 'I didn't come from Canada to go and squat in the jungle. No way. In the school we had fifty early learning books donated from England, two computers from the Germans and three dogs. You think I was going to leave all that for a bunch of Sinhala louts from some godforsaken village in a rain forest? We packed the lot and moved in here. There is an attic at the backside of the roof. You can't see it from the road. We hid there for three weeks eating roti and drinking rainwater. Up and down the street they were fighting like cats: gunfire, mortars, shelling.' She laughed again. 'Our biggest problem was keeping the dogs quiet. But nobody came even near the house. This big, old, haunted house. No Tigers, no soldiers. They were all way too scared of the place.'

'So, it is haunted?' Mahen asked, buoyed up at last. 'A ghost house?'

'If it was, the ghosts also left in the evacuation. It was a fully dead house. Now we will turn it into a *guest* house.' She laughed and opened the biscuit tin. 'You like a ginger nut?'

Mahen grabbed one. Perhaps the caffeine had finally

kicked in too. The father hesitated as if everything in the old country was suddenly suspect.

'No more the school?' he asked.

'Not the same way. I think I will specialize in history lessons. That in itself is becoming a battlefield.'

A bird screeched and a coconut plummeted noisily through the palm fronds and thudded into the ground below the veranda.

'Very dangerous garden,' Dr Ponnampalam said. 'I remember a coconut fell just like that and nearly killed Auntie Matilda. After that my father had to have the nearby trees neutered every season. We had coconut flowers all over the place. But I always ran past those trees in case another nut fell.'

'Those were the good old days.'

'Good?'

'Then, only nuts fell from the sky. When the war came to Jaffna, it was bombs, no?'

'But the house was not bombed, was it?'

'Like I said, in a funny way it is a lucky house. All around the bombs fell on houses, but not here. I think those trees fooled them. Maybe it looks like camouflage from the sky. Maybe they thought it was a chief's camp, so they missed. Those air force planes never hit any Tiger camps however big they were, you know.' She laughed in a big boomy way. 'Safest place, so you don't get bombed, was a chief's place. If the planes came when you were eating at home, you have to run out on the street with your plate of food, because the bombs were sure to fall only on a house or a building easy to see. I suppose they needed a target to aim at like a cross or something, or maybe they just dumped their load when they got tired of looking.'

'I didn't know they bombed all this.' Mahen clearly had not learnt anything in England. Perhaps fathers there said as little as fathers here.

'In those early days, they didn't have high-grade Chinese arsenals. Some of the bombs were just oil barrels filled with explosives, scrap and shit. Sewage. Real stink bombs. So we gave them the names of our favourite government ministers. Here comes the big craphead or there goes the little fart.'

'But now, madam,' I couldn't help intervening again. I didn't want the boy to get the wrong idea. 'It is all different, no? Things are good? No more war, no more explosions, no? New government.'

'True. Much better with no bombs. But you know what they say: even an orange can explode under pressure. So it all depends on what really changes.'

Mahen pressed a finger to the tip of his nose, flattening it. 'You found something here?'

She brightened. 'You know, we are very progressive

here in Jaffna. Whatever the hoo-ha, peace is good. Many of the key posts are now held by women.' She ran through the list: the Government Agent, the Commissioner for Local Government, the Education Officer, the Mayor, et cetera. 'You should stay here with us. You will warm your heart here in Jaffna.'

★

When we got back in the van, father and son were both pensive.

'Back to the hotel, doctor?' I asked.

Dr Ponnampalam checked his watch. 'Can we drive up to the sea? I'd like to see the sea.' His restlessness, I reckon, comes from spending all that time abroad. He was like a foreigner: wanting more and more, even when he had more than he could deal with.

'Which sea, doctor? There is sea all over. This is a peninsula, no? You want the north coast?'

'No, I mean the bay. By the fort. I want to see Kayts and the islands. I remember them, you know. The beach where we'd go for a sea bath.'

I don't think he knew what he was really looking for. He was clutching at fragments in the slow-motion explosion that had been his life. I took the main road that circled the fort. There was a causeway, straight as a needle, connecting the mainland to the nearby islands facing the Palk Strait. I had never been on it.

'Should I go on that?' I asked. There was a checkpoint but another van, like mine, was going through.

'Yes, let's go,' Mahen said with more than a hint of his father's voice.

I stopped by the sentry hut. The soldier peered in but didn't say anything; the language barrier they live with is probably what makes these fellows so tight-lipped up here. He just waved me on.

The road was under repair in places. Very dusty but strangely serene, leading into nothing. A straight road going nowhere. That has been the story of my life. My father never took me to the place where he was born, the village he grew up in. We just stayed where we were by the cemetery in Colombo.

After about ten minutes, we reached the island and a line of trees half submerged by the tide. Marshland. We passed a huge temple.

'This is Kayts,' the doctor said. 'We used to come here on Sundays. It is the loveliest place. They say one of the three Magi sailed from here, you know?'

We came to a crossroads and I slowed down. I couldn't tell a Magi from a magpie.

'Turn right,' the doctor said. 'Let's go into the wetlands first.'

The road was narrower but smooth. A few minutes later, we were in another world. It is hard to believe this was once fighting territory. Trees grew out of the water. Cormorants dived in and out. Wildfowl took flight. A long, flat landscape and a big sky in harmony. There was no sound except for the drone of my van. I could imagine fish idling in the bulrushes. We came to another junction and I turned right again without even asking. Somehow I knew what to do.

'You remember this?' Mahen asked his father.

'Yes, I remember this.'

'I'd like to live here, Dad.'

My heart almost missed a beat. Is this the returning, or the rising of the dead? I saw in my rear-view mirror his father touch his hand as though DNA might be the true politics of the day.

'In Jaffna?'

'In Palm Villa. Can't we rent it from that lady?'

'She is turning it into a guest house.'

'She wants rental, that's all. We can make a deal. Wouldn't you like to go back and live in your old house?'

I saw Dr Ponnampalam flinch.

His son leant closer to him. 'You remember the drawing you did of what you said was our house for my junior school project. You remember? I didn't think it was real. I didn't know what you were on about then.'

I tried to imagine what it was like for him to grow up in a country so far from his father's childhood. Does it make a difference? Are the dreams in the diaspora so very different from ours? I wanted Dr Ponnampalam to say yes. I wanted Mahen to come back and show me how a new generation can build something despite the weaknesses of the old. But then I wondered what he would be like when the gaps in his memory are finally filled and he joins the dots of his and his father's dislocated life. The lives of Madam Sujitha, Milton and all the others dead and alive.

We came to two mangled heaps of rusted iron on a plinth looking like one of those modern sculptures you read about in British Council pamphlets. A soldier was standing on the road next to the enclosure. Further along, there was a shrine with a flag and a big commemorative plaque. Beyond it, the water was still and the sky grey. A small formation of ducks were flying south. I could hear them calling. I rolled down my window. 'What is this?' I asked the soldier.

He shrugged. 'Landmine.' He said it was the scene where, back in 1992, the senior command of the army were blown up. I remembered the stories of plots and counterplots in that era of rage and insanity. The time when it seemed friends became enemies and enemies became friends. But then that's perhaps the way it is, always. Nobody knows who is really who and what they have done and what they might be about to do.

Dr Ponnampalam rubbed his face with both hands, hard and vigorously, as if he was trying to erase something stuck to it. He turned to his son. 'I don't know, son. I don't know if I can. I learnt something, growing up here. It was a refuge once, but even in those days the place seemed haunted. Can you imagine what it would be like to live there now?'

Scrap

I want to learn Chinese. If you are going to live in this country, I think it would be a good idea to learn Chinese. I read in a magazine that China will be the most important and biggest economy in the world soon. It probably already is, because the magazine was an old one at the Belihuloya Rest house. Not really the place you'd go for breaking news. So, maybe wherever you live, even the UK, it might be a good idea to learn Chinese now.

I had four Chinese executives in my van the other day. They might even have been mandarins. Anyway, I learnt three new words: Niha, chi and xie xie. The last is a repeat, so I don't know whether to count it as one or two. And 'chi' means something disgusting to us, rather than 'good balance' as it is to them, so it will be hard to use. Sepala, the guide from the ministry, had to do everything except say 'niha' (hello) and 'xie xie' (thank you) through Chen, the young interpreter from Fuzhou, who had a smiley round face with a pair of pink spectacles pinching his tiny nose. Thirty years of war, sixty-five years of independence, three hundred years of colonialism, two thousand five hundred years of Buddhism . . . Sepala droned on. The whole spiel immediately reverted through the squeaky gullet of this fresh graduate from apparently the most prestigious college of foreign languages in southern China. He was a friendly boy and keen to teach but even keener to learn and already knew more Tamil than I did—although that might have been a blunder in the briefing as far as Sepala was concerned. Tamil cut no ice with him. But he had to admit, the boy was smart. Even before we got to Dambulla, Chen had picked up half a dozen Sinhala words. He said, in rapid-fire English, that his target was fifteen words a day. He wrote them in a little green notebook like an eco-Mao in the making.

'What is the word for "security"?' he asked when we got to Omanthai. And 'minefield' when he spotted the small red skull-and-crossbones signs stuck in the ground.

Sepala was not so keen on the vocabulary Chen

was collecting and kept pointing out the lovely green shoots in the paddy fields, the temples and the new lotus monuments of victory we passed. I tried to give the boy a steer without curbing his enthusiasm. Language plays hell with our politics. Always has. A young mind, like a young heart, is so easy to break.

We were heading for Mullaitivu. I had never been there before. Not many people had in the last thirty years, unless of course you were LTTE cadre, or a local farmer, or one of the 350,000 human shields, IDPs, or what have you, that were shepherded in at the final stage of the war. 'Shepherded' is probably the wrong word, given what happened. But then, shepherds do that sort of thing in the end, don't they, even with lambs? Before that though, before the endgame of the war, this was one of those remote areas where young government officers were sent on their first postings. My last boss, Mr Samarasinghe, said his father spent three years in Mullaitivu before WW II. He had black-and-white photographs of wide open spaces and long clean beaches set like large stamps in a cardboard album which he showed me once. He said they lived like kings, those officers. It is something about this country, I have noticed. We are proud to be a republic, and yet everybody wants to live like a king. Maybe it is the China model. A communist republic where every child, they say, is becoming an emperor.

But a land of a billion can-can emperors is a very far cry from an island of childish hugger-mugger kings.

I listened to Sepala tell his group that Mullaitivu is where our thirty-year war ended and that we are going to see the stock that the LTTE left behind. This was a new kind of tour for me. What stock? I wanted to ask. And why would the Chinese want to see it? But it was not my place to ask and our po-faced delegation did not have any such questions. They nodded and exchanged cool glances. All of them, except for Chen, had that look as though nothing but money would impress them.

We had to go through Kilinochchi and all the way up to Paranthan before we could turn right and head east. The coast was about fifty kilometres away. The Mullaitivu highway is made of flat red earth. I have never been on an unpaved road like it: so wide and straight.

'Who built this road?' I asked Sepala. 'Did the Tigers build this, or is it a British road?

He looked at me aghast. For him, only the government made roads, with a little help from Beijing. The Tigers made trouble and the British had been reduced to penny-pinching tourists or paedophiles. And drivers were meant to drive, not ask questions.

We passed a checkpoint but they didn't stop us. The paddy fields on either side of the road were the brightest green I had ever seen.

Then a mile or two further on, we passed a couple of lorries toppled into a ditch. At the next checkpoint we did have to stop and show our papers, but Sepala had all that sorted.

'Now you will see what we can offer,' he said to Chen, waving a hand and urging him to quickly translate his comment for the delegation.

Big trees shaded the sides of the road. I picked up speed, raising a cloud of red dust behind. I felt I was in a movie. The old-fashioned kind I used to see as a boy at the Regal. Westerns with John Wayne or Rock Hudson. My van was the stagecoach in *Gun Fury*.

A few minutes later, I felt we had slipped into a war-movie set: the trees cleared and we saw fields packed with broken bicycles. There must have been tens of thousands of bicycles in a block half a mile long and twenty feet high. A scrap heap of bicycles. I don't think even in Mao's China there would have been so many piled together like this.

'You see that?' Sepala asked Chen. I slowed down.

Chen leant forward. 'Why bicycles? Why here?'

'Confiscated enemy vehicles. Tigers used them all over the north. Now they are scrap for you.'

Chen spoke to the others in Chinese. I have no idea what he said, but if it was a translation, it seemed to me a little long-winded. Maybe it was to do with the

Tigers. The Chinese, I understand, have a thing about them. The furry kind. Especially their tails and penises. In a quicker translation, I suppose it might all get a bit confused. 'Guerrilla' doesn't help and 'terrorist' is a word that always seems to cause more complications than it is worth. But these are clever people, so I suppose it might have been something deeper.

The next scrap heap on our long straight road was a graveyard for buses, lorries and vans. Some newer than mine, but all crumpled and mangled and toppled over each other.

'Look at the lorries,' Sepala said. 'They used these to ram through our defences and blow up a town. You see the sheets of metal on the insides? All armoured.'

He was right. Some of the lorries had metal sheets for windscreens like rusted eyelids with only a slit for the driver to look through. Such a narrow view, but our visitors were impressed.

There was a hubbub of high notes in the back seat. They must have had currency converters screwed into their skulls.

'A lot of metal here,' Sepala said. 'The sheet metal comes from the hull of a ship they captured. We are going to see it. *Farah-3*. There is a lot of metal for you, if you can collect it.'

Chen frowned and pressed the pink bridge of his

spectacles in with his finger. 'Mr Zhou says if there are many more fields like this, then there might be an economic case. But the problem is that your people will have to get it transported to a harbour. To our scavenger.'

'Can it not come to the coast here? The ship they captured is on the beach. Just waiting in the sand.'

'We cannot bring a scavenger to the beach. It is big, like a tanker.'

'What about your junks? Can't you ferry it all in junks?'

Chen looked baffled.

We passed a row of container trucks with buckled carriages. It seemed as though the transport of a nation had been gathered here and turned to scrap. I have heard that there are places in America and England and Germany where you have mountains of obsolete cars and refrigerators and machines of all kinds, but I can't imagine they are as eerie as this. In our country, if a machine doesn't work, someone hangs on to it and fixes it. They don't get dumped like this. They are always in the limbo of a repair shed. My friend has a car where every component has been salvaged from a different vehicle. He calls it 'Frankenstein's monster' and wants to race it when the Grand Prix comes to Hambantota. But I am afraid war seems to have changed the attitudes of the younger generation. They have become more used to the idea of a disposable society. For them, racing is now all Ferrari and BMW, not the old crocks of yesteryear. This scene gave me hope. It made me think perhaps the desire not to waste runs deep, even in the army. We are the home of Monster Inc.

'These have been brought here, no? Collected, I mean. The owners didn't drive them here, did they?' I asked Sepala. Even if in China they had no questions, I had plenty.

His laugh was more of an ass's whinny. 'You think they parked here? No, Vasantha, this is confiscated property. Stuff the military have captured all over the Vanni and brought here. They have to clean up the place, no? So, now the idea is to recycle it somehow. Mustn't waste, no? Resources on the planet are limited and we are developing a first-class eco policy.'

There were a dozen twisted buses plunged in a flooded field of oily water. Eco policy? What had happened here? We all know something happened, but what? It has nothing to do with conserving resources or green shoots.

A little further on, we came to a crossroads with an information centre. Sepala got down and went to get directions. When he came back, he said we can have a refreshment stop at a military camp. 'We'll go to the swimming pool,' he said brightly. He could be a tour guide for a luxury operator.

Our refreshment stop used to be an LTTE cantonment, but was now a regular army camp. Neat, clean and peaceful. The swimming pool was where the Sea Tigers used to do their workouts. I parked by the cafeteria. The four Chinese gents in their dark business suits fanned out like some mafia formation. Chen in his short-sleeved white shirt and pale chinos looked more like a hostage than an interpreter. I had a wood-apple juice while the others all drank colas. The air was still. But under the camouflage trees, not too hot. The guys behind the bar were all smiling. Maybe because of the mafia, or maybe because of the end of the war. Or maybe it really is just our island's refreshing upbeat style, as the brochures say.

The pool was huge and deep but empty. There was a crack in it. Mr Zhou, the tallest of the group, stood at the edge and contemplated the baby-blue emptiness. He said something in Chinese and the others laughed for the first time. Only Chen didn't. He backed away like a boy afraid of deep water.

'Nothing there now,' I said. I wanted to reassure him. Nothing. Not even water. But he could see that for himself.

★

The road to the beach was another unerringly straight road. I've heard about Roman roads being straight but they couldn't be straighter than this. If that was the way the Romans ruled, then you could see the aspiration here. We passed a church safely tucked under a canopy of trees and a Hindu temple out in the open that had been blown apart. Further on, rows of coconut trees with burnt tops lined the road like tall stumps of blackened fingers accusing the sky.

'You OK?' I asked Chen.

'Sure, sure.' His head tilted, not quite as buoyant as he had been at the start. Perhaps he was too young to know any of the gruesome history of his own homeland. Maybe there they don't talk about the terrors of invasion, the herding of people, the famine, the ideological culling, the suppression of the decent. All that probably disappears in the harmonious joy of economic development. At least that's the idea, I think.

We came to a turning. There was an arrow painted in white. Sepala nodded and I took the corner. If architecture is said to be frozen music, then what was before us was frozen pandemonium. Cars, vans, lorries, buses, cycles, scooters, every kind of vehicle jumbled up and abandoned in creeks and ditches. Whereas the junk fields we had seen before were like a catalogue collection of a mad museum, bizarre but sorted by type and size, this was the headlong rush of a mass of vehicles petrified in the past and whose occupants had vanished.

The set had switched to that of a disaster film and all the actors had been vaporized.

Sepala consulted the paper he had been given and guided me on a zigzag route using hand signals. No words. We drove through what once might have been a settlement or a camp. There were a few shells of buildings, but the rest was random rubble and charred vehicles. The mafia troupe said nothing. Even Chen was reduced to silence. We came to some sand dunes. I followed the road through them and we arrived on the beach.

*

The blue sea glinted three hundred yards away, and the sand stretched as far as one could see to the right and to the left. This, I reckon, must have been the No-Fire Zone, or was it the combat zone? How can you tell: the sand is all pristine white now. I would have asked Sepala, but then dead ahead I saw the huge hulk of a wrecked ship, a monstrous cadaver gnawed through in places and listing in the shallow water with large graffiti sprayed across its rusted broken hull. We all stared, but it was not the most surprising sight.

In front of the ship, out on the sand, about a dozen youngsters were singing and dancing to music thumping out of a silver Pajero. There were a couple of other vehicles nearby that seemed to rock to the beat while a film crew with large cameras and sun shades wheeled about.

'Film location?' Chen asked.

'No, no,' Sepala said. He climbed out slowly. I did too. 'Wait here,' he said to Chen and his bemused delegation, patting the warm air at waist-height like some platoon commander on a raid.

Chen blinked and looked at me.

'Let's see,' I said. When Sepala had started across the sand, I let Chen out and we followed him.

Sepala went up to a young man who was trying to plug his curls into a tiny peaked cap. 'What's going on?' he asked.

'Filming, machang.' He had a clipboard tied to his belt.

'What filming?'

'Pop video, no? What else?'

'You can't do that here?' Sepala swept his hand around to and fro as if to shoo away a bunch of flies.

'Why not? Perfect place, no, machang? If only there was more water on this side of that thing for the girls to jump into, we could shoot them skinny-dipping.'

Sepala's face sagged. 'Do you know where you are? Do you know what this place is?'

The young man took off his cap, and waved it at the long wide beach. 'Amazing, no? So fucking empty.'

'Don't you know what happened here?'

'Happened? Are you talking history? We are the future, machang. The fuckin' A future, no?'

Someone shouted, 'One more take, from the top.' There was another round of top-of-the-voice singing. We retreated to the van. I reckoned if it is pop videos now, tourists must be next.

'They look happy,' Chen said. Of course he was born after the Cultural Revolution in China, after the mad sixties. He was also the future. He couldn't afford to look back if he wanted to make something of himself in the new economic order. But yet, I could see he was a future that still carried questions in his head. I looked back at the van. Mr Zhou and his companions had not moved. They could have been those terracotta warriors turning into news after a thousand years in the tomb of an emperor. They were old men. They must have worn those blue Mao tunics you saw in pictures, and ridden only bicycles once. I wondered whether they still had the old clothes, the old bikes, packed away somewhere with the rest of their revolutionary past.

Or were all those dumped too, and turned to scrap and recycled into iPhones and big fat watches? Is that how it works? If only I could speak Chinese already, I could ask Mr Zhou direct. He looked like a man who had seen stuff like this before. Or maybe not like this, but stuff. Things that happen as our lives move on. I didn't want Chen involved. He was young and eager. He didn't need to know yet.

Roadkill

The first night I stayed in Kilinochchi, I was a little apprehensive. Most of us living in the south had come to think of this town as the nerve centre of terror. As Mr Wahid, my first Malaysian client, said, in English even the name sounded brutal—like the kind of town where you could imagine a Clint Eastwood character striding in and notching the stock of his rifle with yet another senseless killing. In reality, Kilinochchi had been the capital of the Liberation Tigers of Tamil Eelam for years. Here the Tigers had had their civic centre, their secretariat, their press conferences. This was the place where Tiger stamps, LTTE travel passes, GCE school-exam papers, landmines, and black-stripe grenades were issued. The Eelam bank was here, Swiss style, before it came to a swift end in the final stages of the civil war. This was the place the Tigers then destroyed, toppling the water tower and blowing up the municipal buildings, before evacuating into the ever-diminishing jungle as the Sri Lankan army marched in, guns blazing, for the showdown of January 2009.

But now, two years later, I turned off the highway, teeming with road hogs and pot rodents, into the brand-new forecourt of the Spice Garden Inn, and it could have been the latest incarnation of the Colombo Hotel Corporation in full flutter: a northern cousin dolled up with coloured flags, ribbons and streamers. A glass-walled cafeteria shone, and the reception desk overflowed with coconut flowers and bougainvillaea. The scent of wax polish, disinfectant, and karapincha leaves fried in sesame oil masked the lingering spoors of the vanished big cats. This hotel signalled the new era of the old town.

Mrs Arunachalam, who was seven months pregnant and spread across the middle seat of my van, wanted to make the eleven-hour journey to Jaffna in small stages, like an ant on a sugar trail. She ought not to have been travelling at all, the way she sighed and swooned, but her husband was very keen to show her a property in Jaffna that he intended to buy and develop as the new family home, and so she had come.

'Vasantha, can't you go slowly around the bend, please?' she kept saying, in an infuriating refrain, from the moment we left Rajagiriya on her journey of a lifetime.

'Yes, madam,' I'd reply. Yes, yes, yes. I am already around the bleeding bend.

When she saw the flags and streamers, she was jubilant. 'That's the place. That's the place we booked for the night, Kollu. Isn't it pretty?'

Her husband leant forward. 'That's right. You'll be able to rest very quietly here.'

Within half an hour, they had tucked into the best part of a pot of chicken curry and gone to their room upstairs to gently burp and gurgle their antenatal intimacies. By the time I got to the cafeteria, it was empty except for the creepy-crawlies on the wall and one sulky waiter massaging his neck.

'Dinner put.' He pointed at the curry pot and the basin of boiled rice. He was more suited to the job of a traffic policeman, one of the automaton types we used to have before we modernized into a mania for red–amber–green multi-spots.

I took a plate and helped myself to the last bits of scraggy chicken bone and a couple of spoonfuls of rice. I've had worse, but not much worse. One of the things you notice when you drive up and down the country is the variation that's possible in something as simple as boiled rice. Sometimes it feels like you are eating pebbles; other times it's like cotton. At the Spice Garden Inn, the rice was definitely on the rocky side. But after the war and the wall-to-wall fighting in the town, it was hardly surprising that even rice would turn to rubble. The thought of what might have been done with bullets and mortars in this very spot chastened me. I needed a beer.

I asked the waiter for one, wondering idly what kind they'd have: imported Tiger beer?

He disappeared into the back. When he returned, he had a tall, dark bottle of Three Coins on a metal tray and a young woman in a grey trouser suit in tow. Halfway across the room, she overtook him, pushing a metal chair neatly out of the way and coming to a stop in front of my table.

'Welcome.' She parted her lips in a smile, but barely a muscle moved beyond her mouth. Her eyes seemed to be calculating the exact dimensions of my head, neck and chest. She noted the position of my hands and the state of my fingernails. 'From Colombo?'

I nodded. 'Jaffna tour.'

'This is the place to break journey then.'

'That's what they wanted. My party needs a lot of rest.' I patted my stomach as though I was the pregnant one.

'Drivers must rest also. Driving all day is too much, no?'

I shrugged. Once you are in the driver's seat, all that matters is keeping your eyes open. Maybe not all that matters, but the main thing. On these long empty roads going north, even the speed of your reflexes isn't that important. We are no longer at war. 'This is a nice place.'

She looked at me now as if she were trying to tell whether I was being truthful. As if it mattered. 'I am the Assistant Manager. Miss Saraswati. My job is to make this hotel very welcoming so that it becomes the regular stop for *all* tours going up to Jaffna.' She paused. 'For breakfast, lunch, dinner or overnight. We can do everything.'

I had no doubt she could. She seemed very capable, although she definitely needed a better cook.

'Are you from a hotel school then? Catering and management?' People who have made more informed choices in their lives than I have always impress me.

'We had a lot of training.' She let the waiter put the tray down and pour half the bottle of beer into my glass. 'We have to be able to cope with every situation. If we keep focus, we can overcome problems. Any problem.' She had the severe look that some women have when they think that their time is running out.

I waited for the froth to subside. 'Starting something like this up here must be difficult. ETs are pouring into the south like cement from a pipe now, but here it is still only locals, no?'

'Cement?' She looked puzzled. 'ETs?'

'You could say like beer or water, but I was thinking of the new hotels being built and all the European tourists, even the Nordics, now happily sunning themselves on the beach.' As I spoke, it occurred to me that the picture I was painting was probably impossible to imagine in this dumping ground of bombs. I gulped down some beer and poured the rest of the bottle into the glass, realizing too late that out of courtesy I should have offered her some. 'Are you from Kilinochchi?'

'Nearby.' She tipped her head. 'I went to Jaffna and then came here.'

'College?' I asked admiringly.

'Something like that.'

'Because of the—'

'Yes.' The word was quick and oddly unerring. Not only did she have poise and determination but she seemed tightly strung, like one of those ballerinas performing with the Bolshoi on TV. Every look, every movement bound to a larger purpose. The Spice Garden Inn was lucky to have her: it surely would not fail with her in place.

The waiter, who had moved to the back of the room, started. 'Rat,' he yelped.

Miss Saraswati spun around. A big brown rodent was scurrying across the floor toward the tallboy in the far corner. She hissed, loud and sharp, and it froze for a moment. As it began to edge forward again, she grasped my beer bottle by the neck and flung it. The bottle hit the rat with such force that the creature thudded against the wall. The bottle rolled along, unbroken. Its base had smashed the animal's small skull.

'Burn it,' she instructed the waiter. 'Use a plastic bag. Wash your hands afterwards.' She turned to me. 'Sorry about that. I'll bring you another bottle.'

I stared at Miss Saraswati. 'You learn to do that at Jaffna hotel school?'

★

While she went to get another beer, I sat and gazed at my plate of food. I don't mind rats, or the killing of them; I was just a little stunned by her action. The accuracy with which she had thrown the bottle was extraordinary.

When she returned, her polite smile was back in place. 'Sorry,' she said again and placed the new bottle in front of me. She sat down. 'Please eat.'

I pushed my plate away.

'What? No appetite now? Don't worry. It's dead, no?'

'I ate.'

'They are all over the town, but we do not allow them here. I believe it is not good for guests to see.'

'Yes, true. Guests can get upset very easily.'

'Usually the dogs keep the rats away.'

'Dogs are good. Yes.' I had a dog once, a small terrier. It had belonged to a Danish man I worked for in Colombo. When he was posted to Laos, he decided that he couldn't take the little fellow with him. I offered to look after the dog and, when I told him that I lived in a house with a small garden, he let me. But, about a year later, the dog died. It shot out of the gate one day and was hit by a minister's sidekick in one of those high-speed VIP cavalcades on the main road. This happened a long time ago—it was not the fault of our current government— and I wouldn't have told her about it, if she hadn't asked.

She nodded, as though small killings were a natural part of politics as well as of hotel management. She pulled out one of the two paper serviettes from the chrome clip on the table and smoothed it like a mini funeral shroud. 'You have to bury the dead and move on.'

'Bury or burn?'

'That doesn't matter. What matters is what you carry inside.' Her mouth tightened with what I thought was a hint of hurt or anger. She wasn't talking about rats or dogs.

I like to know about the world beyond our shores. About faraway countries where people behave differently. I like to hear about their food and customs. How they deal with the cold and the rain. What it is like to drive on the other side of the road. I like to take foreign tourists around because it gives me a glimpse of a place that is different in touch, taste, smell, sound and look, from the place I am stuck in. I watch how they sit, how they walk, how they talk, and I try to see what they want to escape from and then return to. They are not all driven only by the desire for sex in new places. Some want to know about our history and our culture and what makes us live the way we do. So do I. Sometimes I don't know how we manage. We know so little and the little we do know we get so muddled. Miss Saraswati intrigued me. She seemed to come from some other place: not Kilinochchi, not a Jaffna college, not anywhere nearby but from somewhere dark and hungry and deep. Somewhere beyond the blackness at the end of the garden, where even the moonlight shrank back. Of course, I was not her guide; she was really mine, so the sock was on the wrong foot, if you know what I mean. But still, I wanted to know about her.

'Your family? Are they here?' That might give me a place to start, I thought.

'Have you come to these parts before, Mister Van Driver?'

'Vasantha,' I said and added, 'I have driven up to Jaffna a few times now.'

'Then you must know that it is best not to ask about families. It is best not to ask about someone's brother or father or mother or sister.'

'Why?'

She looked at me like I was a lost cause. 'After a war, it is best not to ask about the past.'

That is not true, I thought. After such a calamity, surely one should? How else will we know what really happened? And if we don't know, will it not be repeated? At any rate, we should not let war, or half-baked political decrees, pervert our native habits of curiosity and easy engagement. But I didn't say any of this. She did not seem in as conversational a mood as she had earlier, and even then she had hovered in some in-between place. Hospitality training, I imagine, helps you to mask your feelings with a smile and to polish that facade of pleasant well-being that Sri Lankans, our foreign visitors tell me, are so good at putting on. But, in Miss Saraswati's case, the training was incomplete. She was not a natural. She could mask but she couldn't do the other thing. She had been named after the goddess of learning, but she seemed to believe that ignorance was bliss. When she turned to look at the door, I noticed a thick scar where the skin had crumpled at the base of her neck. When she turned back, it slid under her collar and was hidden again.

*

In my room in the drivers' quarters, I sat with the door open. Some oil sticks had been lit along the veranda to ward off the mosquitoes. The only sound was the hum of the fluorescent tube further along. Whenever I drive foreign visitors at night, out in the country, they always comment on how dark it is. I used to think, How could it be otherwise? But having been told this so many times, I have begun to see things through their eyes and, for me too, night outside of Colombo now feels very dark. The blackness is like ink seeping through my eyes and into my head. What is happening inside me is no different from what is going on outside. That leads me to thoughts about death, which are pointless and help no one. The difficulty then is to think of something else. Sex, the antidote you grasp for in youth, is less engaging when you are cloistered in a driver's room in the middle of nowhere; and politics, the other base impulse, is a bit of a nightmare these days. Crime—I mean stories about crime, not crime itself—works best, and I especially like crime stories that come from England or America. Bollywood has the edge on musicals, but Pinewood and Hollywood have cornered the criminal stuff. So a pirated DVD is a good solution, if you have the right gadget. I've been thinking about getting one of those portable players; I just need a few big tips to get me into a spending position.

But that night, in the inky blackness in Kilinochchi, all these other things began to merge together: politics, history, even sex, in the form of Miss Saraswati, where it was bound up with mutilation and death. We all have a private past, a store of thoughts, feelings, sensations, disappointments that nobody else will ever unearth. That's just life. But in Miss Saraswati's case, it seemed to me, there was something more deliberately hidden. Areas cordoned off. I suppose it was only natural. So much is kept off limits these days. There are things we don't speak of, things we not only don't remember but carefully forget, places we do not stray into, memories we bury or reshape. That is the way we all live nowadays: driving along a road between hallucination and amnesia. As long as you are moving, you are OK—you have negotiated safe passage, for the moment. It is only when you come to a stop like this, in a black night in the middle of nowhere, that things wobble a bit and you wonder about the purpose of roads. You sit in the dark, frightened at the life you've led and the things you've left undone. You can only hope that in the long run it won't matter, but that in itself is no consolation at all.

The staff quarters of the Spice Garden Inn, or at least the drivers' rooms, had been built by a benevolent but misguided despot. The essentials were there: bed, table, chair, window, coir mat, electric light. The walls were painted. Yellow in my room, green next door. And yet there was something prison-like in the air. The rooms had been designed by a person who would never stay in them himself, or perhaps herself. Each element in itself was inoffensive, and it was difficult to tell what the flaws were. All I knew was the difference I could feel between comfort and discomfort. The ideal and the disillusioning reality. From what I've heard, living in the USSR before perestroika was like that. You knew something was wrong, but you didn't know how to make it right.

I stepped outside for a cigarette. I'm not much of a smoker, but there are times when I have this urge to fill my lungs with poison. If the damage is there, I want to invite it in. Make it mine so that I can do something with it.

Everywhere the edges blurred. I walked along the veranda on a narrow path between light and dark, then out into the garden, where I thought the darkness would consume me, but a tiny glimmer of light from the sky seemed to spread into a silvery web. And when I lit my cigarette, there was more to contend with. After one or two drags, I put it out and waited. Sometimes it feels like the poison is in the air.

Then I saw her. She was on the main balcony of the hotel, a silhouette darker than the darkness, but unmistakably her. Looking out at the fields, like the guardian of an unquenchable dream. She slowly uncrossed her arms and bent down. When she straightened up again, she had something in her hand. It looked like a revolver but when she clicked the catch, a beam of light shot out. She ran it along the fence at the end of the garden and did a sweep around the pond. She caught the eyes of an animal and held the light on it for a few seconds, the beam as steady as a military searchlight. Then she switched it off making the night darker than ever.

★

In the morning, I went and ate some bread and sambol, and waited for the Arunachalams to appear. I took a refill of tea that was a travesty, even by the standards of the previous night's dinner, and sat on one of the garden chairs from where I could see the breakfast room. I wondered how long Miss Saraswati had kept watch from the balcony and when she would resume her office duties.

I heard Mrs Arunachalam before I saw her. She was complaining about her husband's snoring, although I would have guessed that the reality of the bedroom situation was the reverse. Mr Arunachalam said nothing in return. I thought of alerting him to the virtues of the sound-blocking headphones that many of my recent foreign clients sported. They heard nothing that they had not programmed themselves to hear and managed to avoid any pollution of their inner world with the din of local colour. It was an admirable survival technique in a noisy world. Pollution is, after all, the world's biggest problem. Even in Malaysia, people apparently suffer from it.

The couple took a table on the veranda.

'I would like ham and eggs and toast. You think they have ham here?' Mrs Arunachalam scraped her chair forward.

'What about a thosai? Better, no?'

'But I have this craving. And no sleep even, not with you and your trumpeting.'

Miss Saraswati appeared between them and said something I couldn't hear. She seemed able to placate Mrs Arunachalam without recourse to pork. When they had finished breakfast and gone upstairs to pack their toothbrushes and tweezers, or whatever, Miss Saraswati came out to me.

'You are a peacemaker, as well,' I said.

'We do whatever it takes.' She gave me a card. 'Bring all your tours here. We can cater for all.'

'I can see that,' I said. 'Terrific training, your catering college.'

She put her hands together and lowered her head. This time, her collar was tightly buttoned and revealed nothing, but I noticed that the trigger finger of her right hand was callused and discoloured at the edge.

Then Mrs Arunachalam called me. 'Driver, come here. Can you put this bag on the seat in there? I need it right next to me. And put the AC on before we get in, so it will be nice and cool for a change. I can't be getting hot again.'

Miss Saraswati looked at me. I wanted her to smile, even that put-on smile, but her face was blank. Her black eyes gave nothing away. I wished for a moment that I knew what she was thinking, and then I was glad that I didn't. There comes a point when you don't want to know.

Renewals

The guard in the sentry box was grumpy, but that was probably because I woke him with the sound of my horn. Not exactly a trumpet, but it does have an annoyingly high pitch. He rubbed his eye with a fist and studied my number plate. There was nothing to check, only a ritual to go through before he pulled open the gates and let us drive into the library grounds.

The building looked appropriately venerable. Very solid and large and white like something out of the colonial era. But that is all an illusion. The library was burnt in an act of pure malice in 1981 and rebuilt only a few years ago. Even the original building, according to Mr Desmond, was completed only in 1954. Not in the days of the British. So the look is all make-believe—an art we seem to excel at in this country, north and south.

I followed the circular drive to the grand high-ceilinged porch where I deposited my passengers: Mr Desmond and his two assistants.

'You can park around the side,' he said, peering back through the window. 'We will be about an hour.' He may not have been here before but he had studied the plans of this building very thoroughly.

I waited until they had climbed the big steps before easing the van out of the porch. Although technically there was a parking area to the side, as Mr Desmond had indicated, a big metal No-Entry sign blocked the way in so I had to go around the front garden, freshly manured and carefully trimmed with hedges of purple crotons, to slip into the parking area on the other side. The shade trees were huge and must have predated the original building. I imagine the librarians, or architects who designed the place, may well have chosen the site for the trees. Their massive presence gave the place a sense of serenity, even though they had been unable to sustain it against the assaults of our special breed of vandals and lunatics.

There were two other vehicles parked in the shade.

Both cars from a bygone age: a round-hipped Humber and a sharp-finned Hillman. The Humber had a driver asleep at the wheel, while the other car seemed to doze on under-inflated tyres undisturbed by the parrots and the magpies diving in the air above it.

I reversed into a bay littered with tiny yellow jasmine flowers, and angled the van so that I would see Mr Desmond the moment he appeared on the steps. It was not a getaway position really, but it did mean I could move straight in to pick up my clients without delay. Those are the little touches that the big-tour chauffeurs miss but the client always appreciates.

I would have liked to see this library in its heyday. In the sixties, I imagine it was swarming with students. I would like to have been one myself, walking about in long trousers and carrying books and shouting slogans. It was not my life but I think I might have enjoyed it. I like learning. But I guess driving is not something you study in a library or a college, and Tamil was a language I knew nothing of as a boy at school. The Sinhala stream was undiluted in those days. And I had glandular fever as well, which put an end to a lot of youthful dreams of random fornication and dizzy drunken deviations in any language.

On this January afternoon, there was hardly anyone to be seen. I wondered whether this citadel of knowledge was an empty shell. Perhaps there was nothing inside and that was what Mr Desmond was going to remedy. He seemed a man who knew what needed to be done. We need people like that in our country. People who know things and can do things or at least get them done.

As the library was meant to be a place open to all, I thought I should take a look. I have heard it said that it is better to be a laggard than an ignoramus and I had an hour to kill. I locked up the vehicle and went to the entrance.

The front veranda was like something that belonged to a palace. If you went straight in, you would come to a foyer with an information desk. There were two women dealing with inquiries. To go and speak to them, you had to take off your shoes. So I did. The floor was nice and cool. I didn't see Mr Desmond's shoes anywhere but then, being an official visitor, he must have gone straight to an office that did not have such stipulations.

My inquiry was simple: I wanted to know what sort of books they kept in the library.

I asked my question in English. After all, it is the obvious link language.

The older woman replied. 'What are you looking for?'

'Nothing special. I was just curious.'

'If you go up, you can see the periodicals room.' She gestured towards the stairs on the side. 'People like to go there for newspapers and magazines. Go and see. You'll find some old English books there also, if you really want.'

How she had me figured out so easily, I don't know, but that's education for you, I guess.

At the top of the stairs, the first-floor veranda opened into a balcony—the roof of the porch. You could see the sea from there and a good stretch of the road leading up to the library. The big trees on the side seemed less overbearing; one could feel equal to them, even if one was not. A small group of young women in lilac saris entered through the gate. I reckoned they were students. The blob in the sentry box hardly stirred.

*

In the periodicals room, there were a few people buried in newspapers. Older men, old enough to have been sitting in the original rooms of this library before it was set alight. I wondered what it felt like for them to be there, rustling pages in the warm air, hearing birds singing outside again.

Against the walls of the room, there were glass cases with small clusters of old brittle books on thin tindery bones. Not the sort of thing you see in the snazzy bookshops in Colombo nowadays where I have taken tourists craving luscious eye-watering pictures and tasty recipes for hot crab curry and breudher cake.

The glass cases were locked, so I went back out on to the sunny balcony.

'Are you a visitor?' a voice asked me from behind, in Sinhala.

I turned and found a gangly young man sizing me up.

I shrugged. 'I was just looking.'

'What do you think of it?'

'Looks good,' I said.

'They rebuilt it.'

'Is it just as it was?' I asked.

'I never saw it before. I was born after the damage. I only know a lot has been lost.'

I realized he was probably still in his teens. 'I've never been in a library before,' I explained. True. I have taken evening classes and I have read magazines, even books picked up from here and there, but not from a library.

He looked bemused. 'Where are you from? Are there no libraries where you live?'

'I live in Colombo. We have a big public library. Also

the British Council. But I just never thought I could go in. I didn't know they had magazines and all.'

'That's a shame,' he said. 'I come here every day. I am a student. They say this library will one day have a hundred thousand books, like it used to. Even if it does not bring back the poetry, the ola leaves, the record of our civilization and all that, it would still be a day worth waiting for.'

I couldn't imagine a hundred thousand books, or what he really meant, although I remembered the news of the burning. There are all sorts of stories now about who did it, ranging from the cruel to the ludicrous. I suppose that is why you need a record of what really happened. An account you can trust. Or several. And maybe you put them in a library for all to see, and hope no one will tamper with the truth then.

I asked him what he was studying. He said languages: English and Italian.

I felt a twinge of envy. 'You can do that in a college?'

'English at the college. Italian I do on my own. I found a book here in the library.'

'In Italian?'

'Have you heard of Dante? He is a famous Italian poet. I found a book that has his writing in Italian and an English translation below the verses on every page. It is very wonderful. He puts all his enemies in hell. In nine circles of hell.' He widened his eyes and elongated the next words. 'The In-ferno.'

'Is that your plan also?'

'My plan is to go to Italy.'

I tried to imagine this boy in a country neither of us had ever seen and I had only heard of through bits of news on TV, or random conversations about crafty politicos and charming megalomaniacs. 'What do you know of Italy?' I asked.

'I have seen it on the Internet. My cousin sells paintings in Piazza Navona, in Roma. And I have another cousin who is a cook in Sicily.'

'You are serious? You want to leave your home?'

'I have lived here all my life. It has not always been like this.' He pointed at the calm peaceful expanse ahead of us. 'My brother was a hero at the Second Battle of Elephant Pass.'

'The future will be different,' I said.

'I hope so. But for me, the future is another country . . .' His voice trailed off.

One of the young women I had seen coming through the gates earlier had climbed up the stairs. She recognized my companion and smiled.

'Ciao,' he said with a big boyish grin.

She laughed and clutched her parcel of books tighter. She asked him something in Tamil.

'In a minute,' he replied in English.

She rolled her eyes in mock exasperation and went inside to the periodicals room.

The young man turned back to me. 'Only two things here for me now. My Dante book and that girl. The book I know you can download on Google if you have a connection. And she, like me, has no family left alive here.'

★

After the boy followed the girl into the reading room, I returned to the van. I could understand the boy's need to travel, to break out. That is why I have the van. To go places. I like to see things slip pass the window on an open road. But for all the driving I do, I never seem to break out. I am always in the van. And wherever I go in the van, I reach the edge and have to turn back like an ant on a floating leaf. I go everywhere in this country, but nowhere in my mind. Maybe you can never really leave the past behind. It is in your head and outside your control.

When I bought the van, one of the first trips I did was for myself. Not for hire. I went down the Galle Road, heading south. Not to go somewhere I had never been before, but to do exactly the opposite.

To go somewhere I *had* been many times before. To revive a memory not just of the scenery, but the thrill of being there in my own vehicle. To regain the road for myself somehow and bind the past to the present and make it truly my own. I went down the coast like we used to when I was chauffeur to madam and I'd drive her party to Hikkaduwa with boxes of egg sandwiches in the dicky, stopping to buy biscuits from the old Monis Bakery, filling the car with the smell of warm sugar and coconut while the sea played peek-a-boo between the trees and catamarans, and I felt I belonged to a lucky world of free meals and white shirts and iced coffee, where the conversation I could overhear was of a prosperous world somehow within my reach—yes, we had real dreams those days—and I could see the lives of the fishermen through the eyes of my passengers as picturesque rather than desperate and at the mercy of the wind and the waves. What I found when I went on my own was a roadside still littered with the debris of the tsunami, even so many years after that awful Boxing Day in 2004 when the tide played hell.

What was left was rubble, and what had healed was scarred. We have paid a heavy toll, north and south, and now live in the shadowlands forever, mending hope and broken memory as if they were torn nets for lost fishes.

It sometimes frightens me when I think that I can have my hands on the steering wheel, my foot on the pedal, and still be so not in control.

Mr Desmond appeared on the veranda with a lady in a white sari. His two assistants stood behind him while he continued talking. I eased the van forward, giving him time to bring his conversation to a close. I find people tend to rush things the moment they see their transport coming. Only the most confident, and unfortunately the most obnoxious of people, seem to understand that the vehicle and the driver are under their command. A hired car is not like a train running to a timetable. But perhaps we all need a prop, a crutch, an excuse to do what has to be done?

Mr Desmond seemed to have found a decent balance. He acknowledged my arrival, but didn't rush his goodbyes.

'Thank you, Mrs Kumaraswamy. It has been a very useful meeting. I will make sure the books are dispatched immediately.'

One of his assistants opened the door before I could. I tried to shepherd them anyway, as I think it is only right that the driver closes his passenger's door.

I bowed my head to Mrs Kumaraswamy as she struggled to keep her balance on the top step. She was as thin as a stick with a piece of cotton flapping around it. Her eyes wavered. 'We will be waiting,' she said quietly.

I got behind the wheel and we eased out, around the garden to the gate. In his box, the sentry fanned himself with a small pamphlet, and stared as we made our exit.

'Back to the hotel, sir?' I asked.

'Yes, let's go.'

I took a left. The road was clear.

Mr Desmond turned to his assistants. 'You have the list?'

'Yes, sir. All ticked.' One tapped a brown folder.

'We have all those management and technology books from the Americans. They'll like those.' Mr Desmond mopped the back of his neck with a handkerchief. 'And those agricultural development books from the UK. Microfinance and all. That'll do the trick.'

'But she wanted poetry books.' The other assistant's voice faltered.

Mr Desmond snorted. 'Bloody strange woman. I don't know what she is thinking of with that nonsense. Who at a time like this is going to want poetry books?'

'She said something about classics from around the world.'

'Totally batty. She is living so far in the past, you can't even spell it. She said they needed Italian books, for God's sake. Tamil will be tough enough. I don't think she has any idea of what you need these days. How the hell is she going to cope running Internet and all that?'

SOUTH

Ramparts

The lighthouse is always a surprise. So much smaller than you would expect. A sturdy enough how-do-you-do but very much in keeping with the rest of Galle Fort: neat, tidy and erected on a Lilliput scale. Not overbearing like some of the grand edifices that teeter on this risky coast, vast emblems of human folly on the last piece of land in the ocean. From here, there is nothing but water for thousands of miles until the ice of the Antarctic. And yet, this naughty beacon of the south seemed not much more than a paper lantern on a coconut tree.

I had the night off. My three Russians were safely deposited for the evening at a spanking new spa in a fancy hotel. No doubt being waxed and thwacked and mud-slapped even as the muezzin calls from his tower two blocks away. My trips to Galle are the easiest, especially now with the new highway that nobody knows how to use. I love it. Where else in this country can you stay at sixty for more than two minutes? On the southern expressway, I can do it for half an hour. Not even a cat crosses the road. It must be like the autobahn that Mrs Klein from GTZ talked about. No doubt those loose boys in their Ferraris will tear it up soon enough, but I haven't had anyone overtake me so far. In fact, I haven't seen anyone else on it at all except for Simon puttering in his old crock. But once in Galle Fort, when I have parked the van for the night and am taking my stroll down to the ramparts, I feel more like a sailor come home than a driver between runs.

I like to walk from the lighthouse all the way to the very end where the army barracks stand, screened by temple trees with their badly stained blossom. At the end of the day, when the sun is low and melty, the light seeps out in a gold wash and a lovely soft breeze comes in from the sea. Walking along the ramparts, whether it is on the grass bund or the stone walkway, you can leave all the entanglements of daily life behind and slip into a world of your own. Marvel at the luck of being alive in a place so soothing to the soul.

This evening was one of those auspicious ones for

young love. Beyond the mosque and the Muslim College, a stretch of stone and sea invites you to go down to a series of small sandy curves that, like inverted oases, are held between the swirling water and the bays of the old wall. In three consecutive coves, young twirling couples were having their wedding photos taken, fastening their hopes to a confetti of red and gold saris, white suits, black suits, muslin dresses, hats and umbrellas and flowers. Each couple reaching for intimacy but pinched and pulled and clucked and clicked by a control-mad photo-zealot. I have never been married but I have ferried enough wedding parties to know that intimacy is one thing that disappears on the night, even if virginity might have dissolved long before. One must be very besotted not to notice the loss. If I could, I would take all the photographers and their paraphernalia and lock them up to let these couples find the romance they long for, at least for one day, on a real beach of their own rather than in the flurry of images concocted by strangers, which will eventually be relegated to old shoeboxes and obsolete memory sticks.

*

'Match, machang?' A young soldier, in camouflage kit, held up a cigarette delicately between his thumb and two fingers.

I fetched out my I-Love-München lighter. A present from Mrs Klein, who came down here last month looking for sun, samadhi and plush aromatherapy after her Vanni One project in the north. I had been planning to give up smoking, but it was so nice of her that I have delayed the quit-plan and started a pure air deficit reduction plan. And I like the idea of carrying a flame in my pocket. I like to be prepared. In my younger days, I used to always carry a condom in my coin purse, ever-hopeful, until it and all hope completely dried out. A pressed flower or a rosary might have been a better bet, but hindsight is exactly what we don't have in youth, love, war or politics.

I clicked the lighter and the soldier lowered his head to my cupped hand as though I was his confessor. His uniform was not properly done up and you could see the dips around the base of his throat. He also didn't carry a gun, which made me feel safer. There is something about a gun that always puts me on edge, as though the metal has a mind of its own and might decide to burst into action. God knows it happens often enough.

'Nice view.' I said, in Sinhala, making an effort at soldierly small talk.

He checked his watch. 'One hour more. Then back on duty at the barracks.'

'Big camp?'

'Holiday camp,' he smirked. 'After the war, this is our reward.'

I tried to imagine this thin young man with his vulnerable gawky throat diving for cover, shimmying up a hillside, firing a black blunt gun, fighting and killing young men just like himself.

'You have been up north?'

'Five years fighting before the peace. All over, from Mudumalai to Trincomalee. I am waiting to go back.'

'To what? War is finished, no?'

Another wedding couple climbed up on to the ramparts. They stood for a moment against the sky. Their eager snapper popped up like a crab, all angles and bent legs.

'Trinco.' The soldier blew out a slow stream of sweet blue toxic smoke.

'You don't like this honeymoon place?'

'I like it, but it makes me sad.' He waved his cigarette towards the couple.

The gesture was slight, but disquieting. It seemed to cast another shadow over them. I suppose if one had spent years fighting for one's life, then these moments of posed happiness might seem a little fragile.

'This must be very far from what you have been through,' I said.

'It's not that.' He pointed at the barracks. 'Fifteen boys came yesterday. They'd been up in Omanthai, at the border point. Five of them went wild last night, drinking in the bars in town until morning. Three of them snuck straight into bed and the others don't know what to do and just want to go back.'

'Like you?'

'No. They want to go back to the job. To have something to do, you know. It is the biggest problem here. Rest and recuperation is not what they want.' He shrugged. 'At least not the kind that the army can offer.'

'You also want something else?' I asked.

The sound of the young bride's laughter twinkled on the ramparts. The soldier looked at them. 'Have you been married, machang?'

'No, I am a driver. I am never in one place long enough.'

'But what do you think of it? This business of getting married. What all these couples are doing here. What is it about, really? Fucking in a coffin?'

'Two people meet,' I said, 'and learn how to live together.'

'In this country? Is it possible?' He stared at his cigarette as though it were a slow-burning fuse.

'It's not a coffin,' I added, my mind racing. 'The girl and the boy get into a vehicle, a train, a bus, a van, and discover they are going on a journey to the same place.'

'Sometimes people get off early not knowing where they are going. Or get bumped off.'

'Same direction then.'

'Sometimes they meet in a collision.' He dropped the cigarette and ground it with his boot. 'It becomes a disaster.'

Why do soldiers have boots with such long laces? It must take ages to do up. Hardly the most efficient way of preparing a fighting unit. But before I could ask him about the battle benefits of Velcro, he threw me another wide ball.

'Do you think a soldier should marry?'

'I guess you can't live together. In the barracks, I mean. But you have home leave, don't you?'

'What if she is the enemy?'

'The war is over. There are no enemies now, are there?'

'You see my heart is there, in Trinco, in a small red-and-yellow bakery on the bay road where she sells bread and biscuits. But there are these big things between us and I don't know what I can do.'

'Things?'

'It is like a wall dividing us. How can you cross the thing that you have built to protect yourself? Do you know what I mean?'

I put away the lighter. The rampart was a wall. The human heart was something else. 'Does she know how you feel?'

'Her brother was a fighter. LTTE cadre. She doesn't know what happened to him. But I do. What I know is like a stone crushing me, even though what I did was right.'

'What did you do?' I asked.

'We were on our way back to base from Pulmoddai where there had been some trouble. LTTE were doing some nasty things all around. Killing civilians and all. Terrorizing, no? But we fell into a trap. He and three other Tigers were waiting for us on the detour we had to take. A claymore hit the jeep in front of us and then they opened fire. Captain Daminda did a crazy charge and got two of them with a grenade. He was hit in the shoulder but he went on. A real war hero. I got her brother when he tried to make a run for it. I couldn't take my finger off the trigger. I ripped him to shreds. The little shit had killed three of my batch in one go.'

I tried to imagine the carnage. 'How do you know he was her brother?'

The tributaries at the corners of his eyes thickened. 'We try to identify them. I don't know why because I can't imagine anyone really keeping a record. But this one, at least I know who he was. I wish I didn't. He had a photo in his pocket. The family in front of the bakery. She was there in it with him soaked in blood. I got rid of the picture. He shouldn't have been carrying it. I have never told her. It was before the victory but you know how it is. Some things you can't forget. Even if you burn the stuff, the smell sort of sticks to your skin. You can't wash it off.'

★

After the soldier went back to the barracks to do whatever soldiers do on duty at nightfall, I walked back along the ramparts looking at the sea. A dog's mouth. The edge was foaming, the water darkening.

When I was twenty-three, I too had fallen in love. I didn't know it then, but it was the best time for it. The ruptures of '71 had faded and the war to come was as unimaginable as the casual brutality that passes for modern life now. But the social barriers between people still seemed insurmountable.

My father carried golf clubs for a living; her father played with them and probably didn't need a living. I saw her in blue denim, her hair in a ponytail, which in itself was enough to spin my head in 1978. She was careering down the road from the clubhouse in an open-top Mini Moke, the oddest vehicle in Colombo since Dingiri Banda's three-wheel donkey cart. I was smoking by the cemetery wall contemplating life and death in a philosophical sort of way, as we young men who shunned politics for motorcycle maintenance did in those days. The MM slowed for the bend, she changed down and the clutch screeched. Like a toy, the vehicle trundled down to the junction and came to a standstill. The engine was whirring uselessly, the clutch slipping and whining. Flicking my yellow shirt into shape, I went over. Cool as a Sunday ice palam.

'Clutch, missie,' I said. 'It's not catching.'

She looked at me as though I had risen from one of the graves on the other side of the wall, rather than a cool refrigerator. 'Clutch?'

'Shall I take a look?'

'You can fix it?' One of her eyes, beautiful as it was, seemed misaligned. The imperfection gave me hope. I like to fix things, and although I am no surgeon, I am drawn towards the unbalanced.

I opened up the engine compartment and took a look at the clutch cable. I reckoned if I adjusted it, she'd be able to get enough grip on the clutch plate to drive a few miles more.

'How far are you going?' I asked. 'It won't last long.'

'Bambalapitiya,' she said.

'That'll be right,' I said. 'You'll need to call the garage tomorrow. They will have to put a new plate. This one must be ten years old.'

I found a small cloth bag of tools behind the spare wheel. There was a spanner that fitted the lock-nut. There was just enough room to get at it and wedge a fifty-cent piece like a washer.

'Try the clutch pedal. No engine.'

I wondered if I should offer to go with her. I wanted to. I could drive her home, coaxing the clutch an extra mile to take a roundabout route. Maybe catch a glimpse of the sun kissing the sea, together, yellow on blue. It seemed almost possible, but I knew it wasn't. That was not the world we lived in then.

I wiped my hands on the tool bag and fitted everything back in place.

'You have to go easy with the clutch. Try not to stop and start.'

'What? Go without stopping? What about the roundabout?'

'You have to go slow. The clutch is worn out.'

Then she smiled for no reason. Perhaps she did trust me: a cool-hand dude on the road in trousers too big by half. I wanted to say 'I love you' in English like they do in the films. Would she then take me by the hand and ask me to drive her up to Galle Road and over, down one of the Bambalapitiya sea lanes to her neat and polished home of gold coins and cake?

The moment passed. She got in the car, started it and eased the clutch. She knew what she was doing. People like her always do in the end, whatever happens under the bonnet. She drove away with my fifty cents and left me with nothing but a dream.

*

What I like about bringing visitors to Galle Fort is that in the evenings I am almost always free. They rarely need a van once they are settled in their pamper rooms of cosy lust and languor. And I don't have to stay in some dingy drivers' quarters. Most of the smaller poncey hotels don't have staff rooms as every spare inch has to go on water pools or antique Dutch furniture. I have an arrangement with Ismail, another early retiree from the Coconut Corporation in Colombo I used to work at: I kip in his family home where I am given a biriyani dinner, a bed and a simple breakfast for a very modest cost. I only have to telephone him a day or two before and I can be sure of a welcome.

This time I was given the new room that he had added to the top floor. Ismail said that they had just finished it and that I would be the first to use it. After my stroll on the ramparts, I went up to the new room. It had a large window that opened towards the sea. If I leant out, I could see the lighthouse and the ramparts. It made me feel safe—a natural feeling in a fort. After all, that's why they were built. Even in Jaffna fort, it must have felt safe like that once, and here there hasn't been a war since the British beat the Dutch almost two hundred years ago. But I didn't know what I felt safe from: there was no danger that I had to face. Not even a dilemma like the soldier. I felt for him. It seemed to me that he too might miss his chance or not see the turn he should take. Sometimes it feels like we are all driving in the dark with no headlights.

At about 7.30 in the evening, Ismail's son—a boy of about six—knocked on my door and peeped in. He whispered that my food will be ready soon, down in the dining room, and bit his lower lip with a line of tiny teeth. By the time I got downstairs, he had scampered into the kitchen. Ismail was waiting for me.

'You like the new room?' he asked.

I told him it was the best room. The window was a real boon.

'Yes,' he said. 'I thought it would be good to have a window up there facing the sea. I think we will be getting plenty of visitors. Everyone who can is making an extra guest room.'

'I hope I won't be squeezed out,' I said.

'You are the bringer of guests to our town, my friend. So there will always be room for you, Insha'Allah. Who did you bring this time?'

'Russian playboys,' I said. 'They were very excited about a spa weekend.'

Ismail laughed. 'If the walls ever came down in this town, can you imagine what we would see? The things that must go on in those blue steam rooms.'

'The future is in pleasure, they say. One of them was talking about cruise ships coming here soon. You know, big multi-level pleasure palaces with thousands of tourists. They'll eat up the town.'

'We are ready. Open to all the filthy winds of change now.' Ismail laughed. 'We can handle even a plague of locusts.'

I told him about the soldier I had been talking to earlier and how he seemed to feel trapped by the past despite the prospects ahead. 'What could a man in his situation do?' I asked.

'Start afresh,' Ismail said. 'It is hard enough for a woman to really love a killer, never mind the killer of her brother. How can he ever expect her to be his?'

'What? Give up?' It did not sound like the Ismail I knew. Normally, he would be the one who would insist on going the extra mile. If I had known him when I was a young man, I am sure he would have given me the push I needed in front of the Mini Moke, whatever the state of the contents of my purse. He was the one who urged me to go for promotion, to go to English classes, to think ahead. When I retired, he was the one who said, 'Buy the van, Vasantha. Do as you dream.'

He let his eyes droop. 'No, my friend, it is not giving up. But you have to recognize what is insurmountable. To forgive so much is too much.'

'But it was not his fault. It was the war.'

'That is the problem. You have to start somewhere else with a clean slate.'

Out on the ramparts, I had thought that everything we did was an attempt to protect ourselves against the turmoil around us, the sea out there that would dash us to pieces if we did nothing. Our defences have to be strong. But then we find we have become nothing but a line of defence. I wanted to tell the soldier what Ismail had said: start again with a clean slate. Only thing is that I am not sure there are any clean slates left. He might do better just to talk to the girl. Tell her the truth. Tell her what had happened. The truth will come out one day and there was more hope if he spoke than if he stayed silent, adrift. But then, that's easy for me to say. My moment passed long ago. Now I am the one hopelessly adrift.

Fluke

Mr Weerakoon is a smart man with an eye for design. His blue suit is tight so that he looks like he is bursting with energy, which I imagine impresses his clients who are in need of gurus with vitality. His briefcase, which doubles as a computer case, is also blue. Pale blue. To my mind that is less impressive, but it does give him a very modern look like his wedge of shaped black hair. The case is made of pretend leather and has a neoprene sleeve. I know because he told me so.

'Neoprene sleeve inside,' he spluttered, jabbing at the bag. 'Flexible, lightweight, ultra-protection. From Singapore. Good, no?'

He got into the back seat, even though he was my only passenger, saying loudly that he had some preparation to do before the meeting. He opened the case and pulled out a smart silvery laptop before I had closed the door.

I loaded the two cardboard boxes in the back and got behind the wheel. 'AC, sir?' I know now not to take the climate for granted. Sometimes, heading south, passengers can completely surprise you with their eco-preferences and worries about melting ice caps.

'Put it full. Very sticky day.' He checked his watch. 'We have to be there by ten o'clock. You can make it?'

'No problem, sir. Once we pass Moratuwa, traffic will clear.'

'Ten-thirty I do the first session: setting goals, objectives, priorities. After lunch, we do the Plan.' He caught my eyes in the rear-view mirror and grinned. Yesterday Kurunegala, today Kalutara, tomorrow Kirulapone. Boom time, no? Kuala Lumpur is my ultimate goal.'

By the time I got on to Galle Road, he was deep in his screen of bullet points and exploding pie charts. Although I could hear the odd mumbling and the occasional click of a tongue or keyboard, he didn't say anything more to me until we reached the Blue Water turn-off.

He checked his watch again. 'Good timing, Vasantha. Very good.'

I turned in through the massive gates and drove right up to a porch big enough for an aircraft.

When we stopped, Mr Weerakoon zipped up the laptop and patted the bag as if it were a pet. He got out and asked me to bring the boxes I had packed in the back to the meeting room after I had parked the van. 'There will be a big sign: Marketing: The Secret of Success.'

He checked his pockets, patted his blue case again, and waddled down the long straight walkway towards the reception desk in the wide pavilion. He was a man of the modern world. The brand-new face of our remodelled country open at last for full-on business.

★

The meeting room was large and spacious with a view of the pool and the coconut trees around it. You could just about glimpse the sea beyond the steep beach. There were two secretive women and about a dozen shy men milling about near the entrance to the room, several half-throttled by their plump polyester ties. A dumbstruck Buddhist monk—a bhikkhu—in freshly laundered robes stood by a pillar with his tightly furled umbrella, equally speechless.

Mr Weerakoon was inside fiddling with some cables, looking flustered.

I put the boxes on a table by the side. 'Any problem, sir?' I asked.

'Bloody projector doesn't work. I have it all on the computer but there is no connection.'

'Shall I call the technician?'

'He was here, but didn't know what the heck was wrong. Bugger has gone now to look for some jack.'

I am not a computer man, but I do have a knack with machines. Someone once told me that the human body has magnetism in it, and with some people the flow is such that machines respond to their touch, and immediately straighten out the kinks in their system. I took the cables from Mr Weerakoon and jiggled them about. The plugs all fitted their sockets, so I rocked the projector, tipping it one way and then the other. I pressed in the cross-head screws at the back and gave the plastic Ouija board underneath a couple of firm taps. 'Try now, sir,' I said.

He switched it on again and the screen behind him lit up with a picture of a purple bud bursting into flower. He looked back over his shoulder and grinned. 'Bravo! How did you do that?'

'Chinese say you need good chi.' I was pleased to have been able to help.

'You better stay in the room then. Keep that Gucci flowing. Good for you anyway. You might get a tip or two about marketing. You are a small-size entrepreneur, no?'

I reckon neither he nor I could spell the word, never mind pronounce it, but I thanked him nevertheless and asked what I should do with his boxes. He told me to lay out the brochures and the handouts on the side table, next to the coconut cookies. 'My own marketing,' he winked.

A few minutes later the delegates sidled in, shuffling papers and cell phones nervously and choosing their seats around the conference doughnut. Numbers had swelled to more than twenty, but there were still some empty chairs. I perched on a stool at the far end by the boxes where I had a fine view of the pool outside. There was a painted stork standing by it. I couldn't tell if the bird was real. These days it is so hard to spot a fake.

Mr Weerakoon greeted his delegates, bouncing on his toes with the vroom of an enthusiast and then launched into his presentation. The computer worked perfectly and the screenshots faded in and out of flashy diagrams and big bold spinning statements, like paper aeroplanes. Although he said it was about marketing principles applicable to any size of business, it seemed miles too complicated for a one-man/one-van business like mine. The few bits that I could follow seemed to me to be plain common sense: figure out what you want, what your customers want and when they want it. The other stuff about bell curves and market segmentation and www dot shots seemed so much hot air. When I started my business, the whole thing was very simple. I got my pension from the old corporation at fifty-five and decided to do only what I love—drive. I could have got another office job in some private company but who would want to work in Colombo if they didn't have to? That was the time when you had to go through security even for a pee and the building might explode any day with some suicide bomber in a pink sari. No one believed the war would ever really end. So, when Ismail told me that Lionel wanted to get rid of his van—the minibus run had become too competitive for him—and suggested I buy it, I did. I only had to change the colour to blue (because white worries too many people, given all our white van disappearances) and paint a big silver V in English on the side. Then I put the word out at a couple of hotels, the golf club and the offices of my former bosses that I was a man with a van for hire. My marketing was executed in about half the time Mr W took to get his notes in order. Plus a drive around town with a carton of cupcakes for the secretaries, PAs and fixers-at-large. After that, pure patience.

At twelve-thirty exactly, Mr Weerakoon shut the lid of his computer. 'Lunch break,' he announced. 'In the afternoon, we plunge into planning.'

The monk in front of me muttered something about his stomach. The two young women touched each other's wrists and smiled.

Mr Weerakoon beckoned me. 'You wait here until they are all out and then lock the door. My computer we'll keep in here. Safe, no?'

'Yes, sir.' I do whatever my customer wants me to do. That's the key. It is no big secret.

*

On the terrace, by the pool, a special buffet lunch had been laid out especially for the marketing seminar. There was a board on the grass declaring it in big red letters and an exclamation mark.

Mr Weerakoon saw me. 'Locked up?'

'Yes, sir.'

He held out his hand for the key. 'Come then, you can have your lunch with us. We have some no-shows, so there is plenty of food.'

'Thank you, sir,' I said. Nice-looking spread. Rice and curry as well as a creamy stroganoff and something inevitably Chinese with spring onions and black bean sauce.

I helped myself to a spoonful from every dish and sat at a table by the water's edge. The other delegates seemed to break into age groups. The younger men laughed and circled the two women with newfound jargon while the older ones ogled weakly from the coconut bar. One beefish man with a sharp nose and large startled eyes hurried over late from the washroom, shaking water off his hands. He looked hardier than the others and smiled at no one. He helped himself to a heap of rice and stroganoff and came to my table.

'So, how?' he asked.

'Nice and cool,' I said. 'By the water.'

'Yes. Without water we are nothing.'

I tried to fathom it. 'What? Nothing?'

'Sri Lanka is an island. Without water we would just be part of India.'

He had a point. 'But what about Africa?'

His lips tightened. 'Valleys, rifts. No chance. Not Africa. But anyway, we are fortunate to have the sea.' He put his plate down and studied the topography of his food. Then he looked at me. 'Lucky.'

'I suppose so.'

'Lucky,' he said again and stuck out his hand. 'My name is Lucky.'

I stood up and shook his hand, reckoning it was OK. His hands had been thoroughly wet. Washed, I had no doubt, with soap and water. I could smell the sissy lemongrass from the pretty ceramic dispensers in the washrooms. 'I see. I am Vasantha.'

'What's your business?'

'Transport,' I said.

'Mine too, now.' He smirked as though it was a very shady business. 'Water transport.'

He sprinkled salt all over his plate and sat down.

'You mean bowsers or boats?'

He laughed, tipping his head back. 'Very good. Very good.' When his head was level again, his eyes had hardened. 'Navy. We have a fleet parked down the coast.'

'Why marketing, then?' I asked puzzled. 'Is the navy selling stock?' He might have been a naval commander but rank does not bother me. I've had former ministers and high-rolling hoodlums in my van. They are all just punters and in the van they are putty in my hands. I don't give a toss about their social standing or net worth, only their willingness to talk to me. And, very importantly, their personal hygiene. You have to keep the van clean and fresh, otherwise your clients will get put off. No customers, no business. No business, no life. Lemongrass is just the ticket, as far as I am concerned.

'The war is over.' He spoke in a mix of Sinhala and English. 'We have ships doing nothing. So now they have started whale-watching cruises for tourists. Brilliant idea, no? Mirissa is fantastic for it. My concept is to go more comprehensive. They say we have five hundred million bucks in the bank.' He held his fists up in the air as though the money was in them. 'My plan is to persuade the big boys to go into the hotel business as well. Offshore, onshore.' He banged his fists together. 'Connect cruise to hotel and pull the Japanese. Put a casino as well. The rest of the world will follow.'

'The Japanese certainly have a thing about whales, according to an article I read in the newspaper.'

'Exactly. You have to think strategically. If you don't start the fight, you don't get to throw the first punch. Every navy in the world learnt the lesson of Pearl Harbour.'

I hummed my assent, swallowing a mouthful. It made sense. 'You did battles in the navy?'

'Mannar.' His scalp inched back as if at some private marketing folly. 'Very tough.'

'So, you must be happy now. Chasing whales must be better than chasing Sea Tigers.'

He smiled again. 'That's a good one. We should put it on a banner. You are a real marketing guru, no? Yes, whales are much, much better. Everything is good now, except for this stupid WC business.'

I glanced at his hands again. They still looked damp. 'No towels in the washroom?'

'You know, those bloody buggers in Europe and

America want to stick their noses into every little nook and cranny. It is very unsettling.' He swatted a fly that had landed on the edge of the table. He got it. Back-of-the-hand Obama shot. But his face seemed to grow more troubled with every thought. 'Uncertainty is not good, no? Not good for tourism, not good for me, not good for you. We all make mistakes, it is not always a war crime. We have to learn not to scratch at the scabs, no?'

I felt I was getting out of my depth. I finished the last of my stir-fry dollop, Chinafying the stroganoff. 'I think I'll go get some pudding,' I said. 'Nice wattalappam on the side there.'

'You know, we used to have a round bomb that looked just like that. We called it *what'll-happ'n*.' His mouth twitched, signalling another upheaval. 'So, be very careful.'

On my way to the dessert table, Mr Weerakoon caught up with me. 'My phone is gone,' he squealed, all panicky. 'It must have slipped out of my pocket in the van. Can you see if it is there? Brand-new Nokia. It'll be a disaster if it is gone. Big, big disaster.'

I told him not to worry. Cell phones are forever sliding out of pockets in my van. I find them lodged between seats, silted up under the springs, scuttled in the back by the spare tyre. All over the place. Nursing secrets, aching to spill the beans.

Forgoing my pudding, I went to the van and sure enough, it was there nestling at the back with a bottle of mineral water and a packet of cream puffs. The screen was locked but his pin was still the usual four zeros.

By the time I got back, the navy's latest secret weapon for commercial supremacy had settled on a lounger for a snooze. The puddings had been cleared. I managed to grab a plantain off the fruit bowl before that too disappeared, and went to find Mr Weerakoon and give him his phone.

*

I didn't go back into the afternoon session. I wanted to close my eyes out in the open. The others, including the refreshed torpedo and the sated monk, had wandered back into the room to map their future strategies of success in our brave new world of infinite opportunities. There was a soothing sea breeze making music with the trees, the sound of the sea keeping the same soft time it has done since the world began. I wondered what the whales out there in their sea lanes knew of us and our schemes. Even if they had any inkling, would they care?

In the sea air, we can all sleep like old people whose memories have finally receded and left them in peace. That afternoon, under the trees, it seemed as though everything could be forgotten: the trouble brewing under my van, the perforations on the exhaust pipe, the worn treads of the offside rear tyre, the unpaid electricity bill at home waiting for some extra cash flow, that last argument I had with my father, twenty years ago and still knotting my stomach, Mrs Subramaniam's letter I steamed open and decided not to post for her husband's sake. And then, there is everything else that has happened. With luck, one can forget it all, scabs or no scabs. Just float on our unexpected good fortune and snore with the whales—head down in our great comfortable sea of amnesia.

The trick is to learn how to be lulled into sleep. I thought I should tell Mr Weerakoon that, on our way back. Marketing is a doddle. Dealing with a cock-up is the real problem. Small mistakes that grow into bigger ones. God knows we have had plenty of those. A tip from me to him: find out from the sailor how to sleep easy. Whatever your foibles, your wanton misdeeds, you can dream of new ventures and be a success if you can sleep easy. It can't be that difficult. People do it all over the place. A secure pin number is a good start.

Shoot

In the tsunami of 2004, the Galle cricket stadium was destroyed. Obviously, that was not all. Up and down the coast, thirty thousand people lost their lives. Whole towns in the south disappeared. The devastation was as bad as the war. Maybe only half as many people died, or a third, but all in a day rather than over thirty years of human madness.

My father came from a small village near Matara, the southern town that more or less disappeared under the wave. It has now been rebuilt and relocated a few miles uphill. As my father was not much of a family man, and his father even less so, I hardly had any connection to the place and now the place is no longer where it had been. So, that's that really. If I had any allegiance to the south, I would be tempted to relocate it, like the town. Hambantota, not far away, is a luckier spot and tempting. Or, given the vagaries of political fortunes in our country, perhaps I should take a tip from the foreigners I ferry and go for Galle—a magnet since the days of Sinbad. But then, how much of one's life—future, present or past—is really under one's control? Sinbad never knew where he was going. Sinbad was a dodo.

Maybe I should take a lesson from Sanji instead and be more focused on my own needs. As he would say, you must not let yourself drift in some other asshole's shit stream.

*

Sanji was a cameraman. A small fellow with small eyes and a wide nose that seemed squashed from cheek to cheek by the knobbly boxes he pressed against it. Lucky for him that there has been a digital revolution, otherwise he would be completely stunted by the stuff of his trade.

I had brought him to the rebuilt pavilion of the new Galle stadium. He got out warily and laid out an arsenal of photographic equipment in front of the van: tripods, lens bags, cameras, reflectors. Out on the pitch, a solitary groundsman was lining up the stumps.

'They better come soon,' Sanji said. 'Otherwise, we'll have to postpone for the evening.'

'Why?' I asked. 'Nobody else is using the place today.'

Sanji stuck a finger up in the air. 'Sun. After eleven o'clock the light is too damn straight.'

I looked up at the sky trying to imagine arrows of light. 'Is that not good?'

'Very harsh. Wipes out everything. Trouble is that Giorgio says the girls' faces need four hours to firm up, and out here they can't get up at five in the morning.'

I'd seen Giorgio and his girls partying at the rooftop restaurant in the fort, opposite my lodgings, way past midnight. 'Is that what they normally do?'

'In Europe, it doesn't matter. You can work with the light even if you have been popping all night. He doesn't understand how hard it is here.'

'You live in Europe?'

'Milan.'

'I thought you must be from India,' I said.

'Why?'

'You are not Sri Lankan, no?'

His boxer's nose flared. 'I am from Vavuniya,' he said softly.

I usually try to be careful in my assumptions and in what I say. When you deal with people from all over the world, you learn to tread a middle line. But Giorgio and his frolicking poppy girls had confused me. 'You were only talking English, so I thought . . .'

'I speak Tamil also.' He paused. Then he smiled. 'And Italiano. You?'

'Only a few words. I am trying to learn some Tamil. I drive to Jaffna sometimes. My German is better.'

'I would like to see Jaffna again,' he said.

'Maybe your Giorgio will do some filming there.'

'Fashion shoot in the ruins?'

'There are nice places.'

'I know.'

'I mean not damaged.'

'Really? I'd like to see that. I went to college in Jaffna for one year, before joining up.'

I think Sanji enjoyed confounding me. Every time I thought I had his measure, he would say something to throw me off balance. But that's the thing, isn't it? You never know what a man has been up to before you meet him. That hand might only have been waggling his tom-tom, but it might also have been wringing someone's neck.

'Joining? You mean . . .'

'In '83, I was eighteen. I was not a child soldier.'

'How long were you fighting?'

'I was better with a camera than a gun.' His finger was crooked, as if to prove he was more adept at pressing a shutter release than pulling a trigger. 'When the propaganda unit started up, it seemed just the place for me. But then when the Indians came, the politics became bloody Machiavellian.'

'What's that?' I asked, wondering if he had lapsed into Tamil.

He ran his hand like a spider across his thighs. 'You know, all plotting and double-dealing. Indian bloody Peace Keeping crap. It was a game I didn't like. Something had gone wrong. I could see that right at the top people had their own ideas. Personal interests. Your boys and ours were like sprats for their schemes.'

'So you went to Italy?' It sounded like a script to a film.

'I had some connections through the trade. I found some guys and they found me some work. And then Giorgio came to do a documentary on immigrants. That's how I met him. When he moved into fashion, more than ten years ago, he asked me to join his team.' A small smile nicked the corners of his mouth. 'He likes the edge I bring, you know. Fashion also is a kind of jungle. We did London for a few years. Paris. New York. Now we travel all over the world looking for new angles to shoot.'

'Aren't you worried coming back here?'

'The war is over. I am now an Italian. Giorgio wants to break into the Asian market. So we have come to do a taster with cricket.'

'Sports fashion?'

Sanji grinned more broadly, cutting loose. 'We are combining the two niche lines they excel in here.'

'Have you got our cricket stars coming?' That would be a coup, I thought.

'I think they would have liked what we have in mind with the girls, but then the problem is that the selectors, the politicians, every pimp and dingbat will want to be in on the action. And, you know, those cadgers are not at all photogenic, whatever they may think.' He rubbed his fingers together, crisping an imaginary note. 'We only needed permission to use the grounds. He wants a couple of shots at the crease, with the stumps, and a pavilion in the background to contrast with the famous lace here. Our theme is ebony and ivory. Black and white but shot in colour.'

I said I thought that these days everything was done with computers. I had read in a Sunday supplement only a couple of weeks ago about how they can manipulate a picture just like batting an eyelid. That's why nowadays, apparently, you cannot trust any photograph. Nothing is evidence for anything any more. Everything could be doctored. 'That's what they say, no? So, can't you just make it up in a studio?'

He picked up one of the larger long-barrelled cameras and tested it. 'That's not our style. You see, we are dealing with a completely artificial thing. This glamour. So what we try to do is give it some real weight, you know. A bit of flesh. We create a real moment in an unreal world. That's why we need the right location. It is not just in the eye.' He tapped the side of his nose. 'A good photo smells right. If it is fish, it smells of fish. If it is girls, it smells of girls.'

I tried to imagine this small passionate man out in the jungles of the north, filming his ruthless comrades dodging mortars, shooting soldiers, killing innocents no doubt and all the while developing this extraordinary nose that would one day turn him from a fighter into a fashion photographer with the flair of a perfumer.

*

Giorgio turned up at ten-thirty in a swanky new Land Rover. He swung out of the front door, shirtsleeves flapping. He pulled out two cricket bats. 'Ciao, Sanji. All OK?'

Two long slender figures slid out from behind him like mystified gazelles. They wore whites that clung like paint.

One, I guessed, was Italian, the other local or Indian. I am not one to know any more.

'Bellissimo,' Sanji hummed.

The driver of the Land Rover, Mr Wimalasiri from the hotel, got down last, clutching a floppy sun hat.

Sanji put something to his eye and aimed it at the girls. When Giorgio reached us, Sanji wrinkled up his big nose and said, 'Too late, boss.'

Giorgio checked his watch. 'No. We can do it. Two minutes up there, in the middle of the grounds.'

Sanji lifted up a camera. 'The light is white. The costume is white. This is OK for washing powder, not sex in a box.'

Giorgio scowled at him. Mr Wimalasiri seemed nonplussed.

The tiny gold cross on the chain around Giorgio's neck glinted. I wouldn't have thought he was a religious man, but I guess he has the Godfather and all that to contend with in his line of business. 'Girls, strip off. We need you by those sticks out there just in lace.'

'Troppo caldo, Giorgio,' the Italian girl pouted.

'She'll burn,' the other girl whined. The voice was definitely more Bishop's College than Bollywood. 'Even I will burn.'

'I told you girls to wear Factor 50. I gave you the

bottle. Matt finish. We don't want the sweaty look here. This is supercool lingerie.'

'The bottle was vodka, not sunscreen.'

'Never mind. Look, just two minutes is all we need. Sanji here is amazing. He is an action photographer. He can shoot a fucking MiG on speed.'

'Can't we just twirl them around our fingers?' The girl threw back her head in a voluptuous throaty look.

'The point is that the thongs are on you, not off.'

Mr Wimalasiri tried to intervene. 'Just a minute . . .'

'Come on, girls. Let's go.'

Reluctantly, they began to peel off their cling film.

'I say,' Mr Wimalasiri tried again, pointing my way. His eyes, like mine, had popped.

I stared. There was nothing I could do about the sun, the screen, anything. I was here only because the Suleiman Brothers van had broken down and they needed someone in a hurry to bring all the extra equipment down to Galle and I usually take their overflow.

Then the girls glanced in my direction too, which I found disconcerting. I smoothed down my shirt and brushed a hand past my fly, just in case. Slowly I realized that they were not looking at me but at something behind me. I turned and found a throng of schoolboys surging in through the gates.

'What the fuck are they doing here?' Giorgio barked at Mr Wimalasiri.

'Schoolboys,' he said as though they were another species of deer moving through some far-flung Middlesex savannah.

'I know they are fucking schoolboys, but didn't we pay for someone to close this place up for the morning? Can't they lock the goddam gates?'

'Late afternoon would have been better for the light,' Sanji said.

'We were told there would be none of these little wankers here in the morning.'

'School must have closed,' Mr Wimalasiri suggested weakly.

Giorgio looked at Sanji. 'What do we do?'

Sanji squinted up at the sky. Three large clouds like puffs of smoke were drifting in from the sea. He spoke with the cold, calm voice of a veteran. 'We might get some cloud cover for a few minutes. So, you have choice, boss. We forget the wicket shot and give the boys a free show, or come back with pyjamas when the flags are down and the sun is low. You have one minute to decide.' He started to switch the lenses on one of his cameras. There is a point, it seems, when a technician can run the whole show. You have to trust your crew then to know what you want and how best to deliver the goods. That's the way to go these days, in business or in war. Let the dogs loose. Let them do what has to be done. Achieve first, count the cost later. If anyone can be bothered about cost. At any rate, these boys were unlikely to cause any real harm. 'We could do a fantastic chicken rush. Even handheld video, boss, if you want. Those boys look hungry. It will be the real thing.'

'No pads? No gloves?' Beads of perspiration trickled down Giorgio's prickly neck. 'We wanted a finger up.'

'I can do all that later. But this, can't you feel it?' Sanji jerked his head at the mob. It had swelled some more and was beginning to gather speed coming towards us. 'This is the X-factor we have to catch now, boss, or never.'

I could it feel it then, not only out there but in me too as if the urge of the horde had seized me and filled the rifts from adolescence to dotage. The girls looked a little dazed in their tiny slips of lace, unsure of the balance between their magnetic power and their sheer vulnerability.

Giorgio gripped the cricket bats. His eyes twitched as though flicking through the spread he had in his mind. Then his mouth burst. 'Shoot.' He pressed a bat into the hands of each of the girls. 'Both hands, girls. Now run, girls. Run. Sanji, you shoot, you fuckin' shoot the little pricks chasing the lace. Shoot.'

Turtle

Anew road changes the shape of the land. You are, after all, taking a knife to the face of the earth. But more than that, when you cut a new road you change the way everyone sees the place. Our first-ever expressway, for example, a toll road, has turned the whole of the south squarer. Made it more landed. Fair enough you might say with all the baronifying going on, but now we have a route that is solid and unwavering and boring. As more and more people use it, the idea of an island will disappear. If you don't see the sea, how would you know you are on an island? It would only be a rumour, like being at war in some far-off place, or wallowing in indefinite peace, or the idea of the poor coasting idly in a land of plenty, or that the rich suffer equally in times of austerity.

According to Eva, the pinkiest passenger to ever grace my van, and her husband, Pavel, whenever the authorities in the old days of communist Czechoslovakia wanted to flex their muscles, they would build a road. It showed who was in charge and who controlled the destiny of ordinary people. Except, of course, they eventually lost control and missed destiny by a mile. Now who even remembers the name of Gustáv Husák, except those who had the misfortune of living under his thumb? And people like me, I guess, with time on our hands, twiddling our thumbs behind a wheel.

'How did that happen?' I asked.

'Our Velvet Revolution,' Pavel said with an enigmatic smile. 'It changed the world.' He didn't speak as much as his wife, but whenever he did, he also forced a smile. He had neat straight teeth. Dental care must have been very good when he was a child. Communism, even behind the rusty iron curtain, couldn't have been all bad if your teeth were kept in shape like that, and for free. They used to say you could tell a lot about the quality of life for the ordinary person by the state of the nation's teeth and his was a lot better than any you'd see in a comparable mouth here or, I bet, even in America.

'I remember something about the iron hand in control.' I said. 'It was a phrase, no?'

'The invisible hand?' Eva suggested, blowing a bit of stray floss back.

Her husband dissented. 'No, no. That is now. Capitalism is the invisible hand we have clasped to our hearts, my dearest. Then, before 1989, we had iron fists shoved in our mouths. We had blinkered eyes and concrete heads.' He let a small laugh escape the ivory cage. 'It was a bad time.'

'You cannot imagine it, Va-shantha,' Eva said, struggling sweetly with my name and whistling as she spoke between her even more beautifully proportioned pearly gates. 'They controlled everything and sometimes very harshly, but also sometimes very subtly. Like the iron fist was in a velvet glove.'

'I have heard that saying also,' I said.

'Life was better than in many other countries behind the curtain, but censorship made it difficult for us to speak, you know,' she added as though it was a matter of dental hygiene.

'Strangulation, but done cleverly. They left no external marks.' Pavel felt his throat. 'As a country, we almost stopped speaking altogether.'

'Everything had to have a double meaning otherwise there was no meaning.' Eva put her palms together and opened them like a book of flesh. Her small breasts heaved and she oozed a scent that made me think the hand gesture must be from an east European Kama Sutra or something.

'But English then? How did you learn English?' I asked, trying to banish the unnerving image of her strapped to a dentist's velvet bed with her lovely lips bared.

'We all learnt as many languages as we could. It made up for the silence around us.' She shook her pale hair to free her head from the old days. 'Our theatres used silence, our artists used darkness, our writers used the surreal, symbols, double entendres. That was the way to speak about things. That, and using foreign languages. Anything but Russian.'

It made sense.

When I turned off the pristine expressway on to the old coast road, my passengers both sighed in unison at the sight of the sea. Dirty grey and choppy in a ruffled bay but still a real bit of ocean as you would rightly expect to see around an island, silent or not.

Eva murmured, 'That is beautiful.'

Her husband stroked the long-haul fuzz purpling his jaw. 'Now it feels like we have really arrived somewhere new. The highway was like driving to Brno. But this is what we imagined when they said, escape to paradise.'

It is amazing what a splash of water can do. No wonder people go mad in a desert. I used to think a mirage was an illusion, a mistake, brought on by the pressure of a hostile environment, but now I wonder whether it is really a strategy for survival. Something we make up because we need to, because the alternative is a reality too hopeless to live with. Travelling, even loafing about, is I guess one way of making it up.

The couple had been booked into the Green Shell, a boutique hotel further down the coast. I had never been there before but I had the exact paper coordinates.

Further down the old-style coast road we came to the more seductive curves of the south. The glimpses of sand, the swish and skirts of the smiley sea, entranced my passengers and they seemed to drift into a dreamworld just like the rest of us. After about half an hour, we reached the specified marker. The hotel had high daunting iron gates painted a lizardy green. I honked the horn and the gates opened. I drove up a gravel drive. In front of us a lush vivid garden rippled out. Grey columns or pillars, which I call 'Bawa lines' (after a lesson on architecture from one of my first tours with Mr Dissanayake), rose to long sloping green roofs spread like wings pinned in flight.

'It's beautiful,' Eva said again, making me wonder if her English was more limited than I had thought.

'A castle by the sea,' her husband added.

I opened the van and got their colour-matched leathery luggage out. A young man in a green sarong appeared at the entrance and smiled one of those large lopsided smiles, like a split coconut, which dazzle our visitors into forking out fistfuls of money for trifles and curd. He stood there as though that was all he needed to do in the business of hospitality: smile timelessly and wait for a tip. Service at the Green Shell, it seemed, was discreet to the point of neglect.

'Bags,' I snapped at him and that woke him up.

Pavel reached out to shake my hand. 'Thank you.'

It might have been a legacy of his communist upbringing, or sea-air amnesia that brought on this act of leave-taking, but we were not due to part company yet. There was no need for handshaking. I had been hired for the week: two nights on the coast for some steamy moonlight and sea spray, then a shopping day in Colombo before a romp around the hill country and our inescapable cultural triangle. In any case, the obligatory scented wet towel rolls hadn't been brought to freshen up and clean our hands. So I smiled too, like a good local, and kept my hands to myself.

The couple went up the steps more tentatively than most of my other foreign tourists would. These two had soft crepe mules on, with white socks, and they walked as though they were mice in a Moscow ballroom rather than a couple girding their loins for a strenuous bout of honey spooning. Usually, even at this stage of a holiday, four hours off the plane, most of my European clients would have abandoned all footwear and be flopping around vastly unbuttoned, swinging giddily between the sudden prospect of loose liaisons and the unexpected handicap of blistering heat. Not these two. Perhaps they had never seen the sea so close and the sea you could glimpse from the foyer was like a blue whale in clover, or something.

I followed them and stood nearby in case they needed my help to negotiate things. I like to do that little bit more for my clients. It's the way to build a proper business.

The manager, who looked much more the tourist in his green shorts and flowery shirt, stepped out of his office and also did the local smile. Even his flip-flops were green. His big yellow toes pricked up as he shook his new guest's still loose aimless hand which clearly made Pavel feel much more at home. More so, when the manager added to his greeting, 'Dobrý den!'

Pavel didn't let go of the hand. He pulled the man nearer and searched his face. 'Ĉeský?'

The manager grinned disarmingly and broke free. 'Slovakia, actually,' he continued in English. 'Welcome to the Green Shell. Please, have a cool drink.' He beckoned a dazed-looking girl who floated up carrying a tray of long cloudy glasses decorated with fruit ribbons.

They say this island of ours is the crossroads of the world. A lot of blah-blah about trade routes, sea lanes, strategic points, et cetera. But the more I see of it in this business, and the more people I meet, the more I understand the real truth of the matter. We live at one of those crazy junctions where everyone gets stranded not knowing which way to look, never mind go. All nodding like sleepyheads unable to ever completely wake up.

*

Late in the afternoon, after a cup of trendy green tea, I came out to watch the sunset. I don't know why we are always drawn to it. Moths to a flame? Or maybe we are just fascinated by the idea of an end; the horizon and what lies beyond the finishing line. I've heard that only the human species thinks about their own demise, and maybe that's what it is, but we are not the only ones prone to self-destruct. Who knows what the moth thinks? At the boundary of the garden there is a bundy roll of grass. Beyond that a short steep beach and then the huge sea sucking at the sun. Standing at the edge of the sand, you cannot help but be mesmerized. Although I know that it is the earth that is turning and that this drama of a sinking sun is only an optical illusion, it is hard to believe that the sea is not pulling it in and that we are not witnessing the death of a god. A sun god that bends down to kiss his own reflection, and in so doing dies. Again and again.

'It is so beautiful.' Eva had come up behind me. 'The sea is beautiful.'

'Yes, madam,' I agreed. It was beautiful in a terrifying sort of way. I couldn't get the death of the sun out of my head. They say it will happen for real, millions of years from now. But when it happens, would it be at dusk? On a day like this? It sinks. Touches the sea. And we all go out like candles nodding in a dark silent gale, grasping for a last word.

'We have come a long way for this,' Eva said sleepily. She ran a blue shawl through her fingers. I am no Hindu, but the blue rush made me think of Krishna blooming under the milky hands of a gopi.

'The sunset?'

'A place so beautiful you can forget everything.'

'Where do you live, madam? Is it what they call a concrete jungle?' I stuck to my protocol.

'No, we live in a very pretty place. A city by the sea.'

'I thought Mr Pavel said you had no sea.'

'That's in our homeland. But for the last few years we have lived in Croatia. He is working there. We have the Adriatic near.' She hesitated a moment. The wind lifted and the thousands of leaves and fronds in the garden made a collective sound to muffle my pulse. 'But there are difficulties.'

'Croatia has had some trouble, no?'

'The history is not so nice,' she said staring steadily ahead. 'We have come to forget what he has to do there.'

'His work?' It baffles me, what some people do for a living and what they do when they don't do that.

'Yes, but I have been thinking of nothing but that. The loose memories. The nightmares of those who were children in the war. What good could possibly come from such bad happenings. We thought at least we won't have to talk about it here. We have agreed not to mention it to each other.' She raised her bare coy shoulders. 'He and I,' she added, and I wondered whether that meant she would like to talk to someone else about it. That she would like me to ask her about her life and what had become of it.

So I did. 'You like your home country more than where you live now, even with the sea there?'

'Yes. I do.'

'Where is that home?'

She looked down at her feet, searching for a clue. 'A small town near Prague. Nothing there but fields and a forest full of fungi. We had a famous explosives factory but that is closed now.'

I wondered if she could see how closely we might be connected: the fuse that quite possibly wired her parish arsenal to the young woman who blew herself up in front of our office building in Colombo only a few years ago. 'You grew up there?'

'Yes, I never went anywhere until I went to Prague. To the university. I met Pavel there. He comes from Zámrsk. Also a small place, but he knew much more about the rest of the world. His father had even come here to Ceylon in the 1960s as an engineer on some construction project. "Solidarity through technical assistance" was the slogan those days. We had a song about that in school.'

'Mr Pavel came too?' It was like one mad thing after another.

'No, he was not even born then. But he wants to find the house where his father stayed in Colombo. The tour operator recommended we spend at least two nights here first, by the sea, to relax, you know, before going to the city.'

'That seems to be the recommended itinerary these days, for honeymooning especially. With the new road, it is all now easy.'

'I am so glad to be here. I don't need to go anywhere else. Here I think I might be able to forget everything. It feels safe.' She glanced at me. 'Do you also think it is safe?'

At that moment, I did not feel I was in the safest of places. Not with her floating so dreamily in an ocean of emotion.

The sea, it is true, can be sleepifying, but even then to my mind it is not very safe. Maybe it is because I am a driver, and I need to guard against the forces of narcolepsy. I read an article about that in *Reader's Digest*. The sound of waves, lullabies, popular songs, things that soothe too much and put you to sleep behind the wheel are very dangerous. Apparently, it is a big problem on the highways of America and Europe, although I guess they don't mean the rhythm of the sea but radio waves, or country music. Still, the same applies. But I didn't want to spoil her mood with my dark thoughts.

'The boys here say that turtles find this spot the safest. They come up the beach every night.'

'Really? This beach here?'

'Yes. They come to lay their eggs. If you are lucky, you'll be able to see them tonight.'

Perhaps it was the wind, or the sharp stingy air, but her eyes seemed to moisten. It struck me then that quite a few of the foreign couples I drive to the coast, and up and down the hill country, have a similar urge. They come eager for a wedding ritual, or a second try at the honeymoon, yearning for the nuptials of a lifetime in the warm air. They come propelled from the inside to perpetuate their dreams and then are dumbfounded. Eva seemed to me to be a woman at that vulnerable age when one's urges ripen too fast to know what to do.

'You must watch the sunset first,' I added. 'When the sun goes in the water, there is a green flash. If you make a wish when you see it, the wish will come true.'

'Really?' For a brief moment, it looked to me as though the green flash was in her eyes.

'That's what they say.' I shrugged. 'Never worked for me, but I find it very difficult to keep the wish in mind while looking so hard to see the green flash.' The truth dawned on me then. 'Actually, maybe it does work, because at the moment you see it, you realize what you have been really wishing for is only to see it. Nothing else.'

She smiled at that. 'I will give it a try.'

Behind us there was the whoosh of green water parting in the pool. Pavel hauled himself out and picked up a striped towel from one of the deckchairs. He draped it around him and came towards us. His belly hung low and heavy and was streaked with long hair. He looked like a bear in wet pyjamas.

I stepped aside.

He patted his wife's bottom with his paw. She brushed it away.

'We have to watch the sun go down,' she said.

I left them to it. Wishes are a risky business. That's one thing I have learnt for sure in these last few years of war and terror, of unexpected peace and pockets of prosperity. The risk of unintended consequences is always very high.

★

The owner of the Green Shell hotel was a Gujarati from Dubai. The cook at the back was the only animated creature in the whole establishment, but he didn't know much more than the name of the man—Mr Bharat. He said Mr Bharat appears twice a year when there are things happening in Galle and when he has special guests. The rest of the time he lets Alex, the manager, run the place anyway he likes. Some weeks in the low season when it is too hot and there are no guests, all the staff sleep in their sarongs by the pool, snoring with the trees. All except the cook. If no guests are booked, he says, he goes home to his family. Nobody ever just drops in. It is not that kind of a hotel. If a reservation is made, out of the blue, Alex calls him on his cell phone and he cycles over.

When Mr Bharat comes, it is a different matter. Everyone wakes up, the cook said. It is like they all get an injection in the butt. The gardener is out sweeping the grass, the room boys are dusting from floor to ceiling, rubbing the salt off every strip of wood, the receptionist is on the phone organizing the world and its uncle, and even the accountant is jumping from ledger to ledger like a cat on gas. Only Alex continues unchanged. Smiling like there is no tomorrow, high on something or the other.

As it turned out, on this February night, Eva and Pavel were the only guests. For dinner, Alex had organized a candlelit table in the central veranda with small temple lamps circling it on the floor. You could hear the sea, and the green sleeves in the wind. Nothing else. I finished my meal early, in the staff quarters, and strolled out into the garden where halogen mushrooms had blossomed in a forest of shadows. I saw the couple at their table. They had a bottle of wine in a silver ice bucket on a stand next to them and sparkling wine glasses close to their lips. They had asked for seafood, and the cook had decided to make a squid dish with coconut, sea kale and kankun. Chancy for a first night, in my opinion, sea or no sea. I was tempted to ask what they thought of the creation but I didn't want to intrude. They had their fingers intertwined and their ankles were touching, reddening under the table. I walked by the edge of the pool instead and went up to the beach.

In the dark, the sea seemed a troubled creature coiling and swirling and slapping its washing on the sand. The nightwatchman was out by one of the gateposts. He had a flashlight in his hand and a gun in a holster on his hip.

'What's it like here?' I asked him in Sinhala.

'Good.' He moved a piece of driftwood out of the way. 'Now it is good.'

'Why the gun?'

He checked the holster. 'We had some trouble once. But not any more. Not after the boss arranged this little putha.'

'What kind of trouble?' I asked.

'All kinds, but not now. Nobody dares to come near this hotel after I fired a couple of shots.'

'Only turtles, huh?'

'Yes. They come. Every night at this time of the year. You'll see them any minute now.'

I took some foreigners—friends of my boss in those days when I worked at the corporation—to a turtle hatchery once: that was before the tsunami. Such frail little things piddling in a tank, you couldn't imagine how they would grow those huge shells and end up looking like humps of rock.

'They have their favourite spots on the beach?'

'I don't know if they are the same turtles, but they come to the same places.'

'Maybe they have memories just like us.'

The nightwatchman laughed. He had a slippery laugh

that skimmed the water like a flat stone. 'They are smarter than us. Their memories they pass from generation to generation.'

'I think we do too,' I said. I don't know why I said it. How would I know? It was just instinct. I think I was thinking too much about the troubles we have had, year after year, wave after wave. There was a time it seemed it would never end.

Eva and Pavel came up arm in arm, halfway between stuffed to bust and conjugal cohesion. 'Are they here? The turtles?' She loosened herself from him and swayed closer to me. I could smell grape on her breath, or a cocktail of something more carnal.

'No,' I said. 'We haven't seen anything yet.'

'Alex said they would be on the beach by now.'

The nightwatchman swung his flashlight and the beam swept the sloping sand, dancing over the suds draining out.

'I missed the green flash at sunset, so I have to see the turtle,' Eva teetered on tiptoe. 'Isn't it also good luck to see a turtle?'

'So they say, miss,' the nightwatchman said. 'That's what they say, but if it is true I must be the luckiest man in the world.'

'You are,' she laughed tipsily. 'Amazingly lucky to be here every night.'

I saw Pavel's teeth gleam in the moonlight.

'Lucky, miss?' The nightwatchman lowered his head. For him, on his beach, it seemed there was only the pounding of the sea. A deep, dark, unrelenting sea. 'Maybe, miss.'

'Sure. Just look at all this.' She flung out her hands. 'The Indian Ocean.'

'Yes, miss. Like you say, I am lucky to be here.' He paused, not sure whether he should disturb the eager couple with any more talk about himself. Then, as if unable to stop the flow, he added, softly, 'I survived the tsunami.'

I heard her take a sharp breath. 'Here?'

'Just nearby.' He switched the flashlight on again and indicated the mean curve of the beach. 'We had a house over there. It went with the wave. They all went, my wife, my daughter, my son, my mother, my brother and all his family and my uncle's family. All twenty-two of them. All except me. Big bad wave.'

The breeze dropped. The sea seemed to have flattened before his words. Nothing broke the surface. No turtle heads bobbing up. There were no flippered domes on the wet sand. No sign of them at all. You'd think there was no life left anywhere in the water.

'I am so sorry,' Eva said, standing very still.

Right at the edge of the horizon, I could see the tiny yellow light of a fishing boat.

'But you are right, miss,' the man said. He kicked some sand down towards the sea. 'In this world, we must be the lucky ones if we survive from one day to the next.'

Janus

We know about Stalin now, we know a lot about him and his ruthlessness. We know all about his blind spots. His folly, his mistakes with Germany, his mad collectivization. We also know a lot about Mao's blindness: the Great Leap into a hole, the Cultural Revolution. Great leaders make great mistakes. It is a sort of status symbol that they cannot resist. We can see it in our own day, all over the world from UK to Ukraine. Italy to Iraq. My father used to say: make big mistakes, make big history.

His own were minor, so nobody knew about them except me and a bunch of his old cronies who have now all passed away. Mistakes of not seeing things for what they were. He admired strategy and would draw comparisons between Bismarck and Khrushchev, as though ships and shoes were the same thing. Or Gandhi and Rommel as if they were brothers and the salt march was a desert fox's false trail. In the world of the Royal Colombo Golf Club where he worked as a caddie, he was an intellectual giant. A self-taught revolutionary political force bursting into consciousness in a wilderness of Crimplene slacks and muddy water holes. He didn't see that his own life was of such little consequence that his name would be forgotten before the ninth hole: 'Oi, caddie, what to bugger that with now?' his golfers would ask, eyeing the rough, the pin and the lie of the land. One time he tried to organize his fellow caddies to demand better conditions and a rise in pay rates. A reasonable enough project, you'd think, but he picked a fight with some four-iron thug who wouldn't budge, instead of asking to meet with the committee in the clubhouse counting the dosh. His errors were peanuts but they pained him. 'A good man will not forget even a misplaced divot,' he would say, 'whatever the state of his front yard.' But big shots are just brazen. When a big man takes a wrong turning, he doesn't back out like you and me, he just tears up the whole road and makes a new map. Nobody knows what to do then. And if he barges about with enough bravado, he can be a real hero.

Take Brigadier Bling. Despite looking like a shrunken version of Lenin—the forehead a little deflated, the chin knocked back in an upper cut—he had become the most popular figure on Colombo's five-star dance floors during the war. He was often pictured in the society pages of the glamour magazines, in a champagne handloom kit and silver cuffs, with a canyon of glossy flesh on high heels purring above him, grinning as if he'd tripped out of a Soviet time warp into our local Neverland. He became a celebrity after blowing up a cave in Kurunilpitiya where the Tiger chief was meant to be doing an early Saddam. The whole thing had misfired and the subsequent Tiger retaliation had been brutal with massive not-so-collateral damage, but he had nailed two second-tier enemy warlords in the aftermath and managed to get the TV cameras in for the victory parade. Next thing you know he is the daily news in full regalia with the epaulettes blooming on his shoulders: a champ and a star.

I recognized him the moment he stepped out of his buggered-up black Peugeot on the side of the old Galle Road. The car had its nose to the ground and the driver who flagged me down was a soldier with a gun.

'Take the sir to Ambalangoda,' he ordered.

'What happened?'

'Bullock,' he said. 'As we came round that shit bend.'

I saw the creature then, hooves in the air, head in a ditch. 'So, army has no backup now?'

'Shut up and take him to Manel Guest House. The turn-off is at the 84 kil-stone.'

'Guest house?'

'Right.'

'Not five-star?'

'Just do as you are told, mister van man.'

I had dropped off two Iranian New Age anglers at an emporium in Hikkaduwa on a one-way run (although they had properly paid for the full return fare) and was on my way home, so it was not a problem. In any case, unlike my father, I knew who you shouldn't argue with. Armed soldiers were at the top of the list, next to policemen and ministers of state, not counting kingpins and top dogs, of course, who could wallop you any time they chose.

The soldier slid the door open and the brigadier climbed in. His face was sombre, his moustache dyed but droopy. His was a face that clearly brightened only for a camera, and preferably after a cocktail or a quick jig had eased the pain of snuffing chaps. I released the brake and got going. Although he was a big man in the military, he was now firstly my passenger. And in the van, I can pull rank. The captain of the ship is the boss. At any rate, he was not in uniform—except for his boots—and although he wore three rings close to his knuckles and a huge watch, he had no gun.

From all the antiterrorism measures we've been through, I know the importance of establishing authority in times of upheaval. So I said, 'Sir, please fasten the seat belt.'

He didn't protest as some big shots like to do. I heard the click of the buckle. My mind was racing. This was one helluva pickup, I thought. You don't get to ferry a man like this very easily as a free agent in the business. Heat-seeking tourists in a daze, home-seeking desperadoes from the diaspora, freewheelers and business-seekers from erratic states, these are easy pickups, but a guy who can do a killer foxtrot and the Gaga jive with equal ease, and whose career from the battlefield to the ballroom was legendary, is a gift from the gods. In 1958, my father was drawn as the caddie for Didi Singh, the champion of Dehradun and the most elegant swing in the southern hemisphere of his era. He said it was 'a gift from the gods' just to watch the man walk and, for a barefoot communist atheist like my father, that was saying something. Now I knew what he had meant: by sheer chance to be in such close proximity to a superstar was not to be sneezed at whichever way the wind was blowing.

I didn't say anything else for a couple of K's. I let him settle in and become comfortable in the van. When the road is clear, the steady drone of the engine and the sleepy road humps that swell a long-distance journey lulls everyone into that couch-state, which allows dreams to drift out of their mouths. I too go into a state, but I have to be sufficiently alert to avoid stray cattle and gunmen, and that I have learnt to do. Driving a van is not like driving a tank. There is an art to keeping things smooth, to listening, and to learning the ways of the world we live in.

'Is it a dance?' I asked after a little while.

'What?'

'This place in Ambalangoda, is it like for a beach gala you are going?' I realized my mistake the moment I said it. He was not a holidaymaker and being so direct may not have been the most productive line to take with a man sharpened by military manoeuvres and jive talking. I tried to cover up with blather. I told him how I knew of a very talented mask-maker in that area who has diversified into making costumes for celebrations and galas. I said I had heard that Ambalangoda beach parties had become very popular with the fashionable set in Colombo and that was why I thought he might be going there. Given his reputation, I reckoned he might be game for a devil-mask.

But he said nothing. His face was as good as a mask. Unlike him, I sometimes don't know how to keep my mouth shut. I get that from my father. He also had the knack for speaking out of turn.

'You know, sir,' I said, 'now that the war is finished, you can get all your soldiers doing salsa or something, no? Instead of that goose-step business on Galle Face we could have a carnival like in Cuba or somewhere.' I had heard that even Castro liked to tap his toe and I thought a Mardi Gras of the Buena Vista might have more appeal than a Kim Jong-il parade for the brigadier, but he still said nothing in reply.

*

Manel Guest House had little to distinguish it from a hundred other seaside houses dotted along the coast. Even the lettering of the signboard was the same as any other place with a room or two to let. In the front, facing the road, a new wall had been built with barbed wire on top. An odd precaution, I thought, given that the tsunami sea on the other side of the house was surely the real danger these days.

I beeped my horn at the gate and waited.

A wire-haired old woman opened it and ushered us in.

The brigadier stepped out of the van as though he were at a sunset drill. I am sure his hand brushed his forehead in a half-salute, but I suppose it might have been something more traditionally deferential towards the old housekeeper. I watched unsure what I should do next. My mission was accomplished: I had delivered him to his destination. I must therefore now be a free man. But with the military, even in civilian clothes, you couldn't take such freedoms for granted. So I asked the brigadier point-blank. 'This is the place, no? OK if I go now?'

He looked at me as though I might make a good target for rifle practice, or even a bayonet run for one of his young machine heads, but he spoke politely. 'Can you wait a little? Have a cup of tea. I am sure you need a cup of tea.'

The old woman put a wrinkled hand to her mouth. She seemed to be laughing but with no real mirth. 'One sugar, two sugar?'

'One,' I said, brave as any runt of a soldier in an ambush.

They both disappeared and I waited by the van. The house had a modern airy look: a pretty front door, punctured with fretwork, was set in a wall of curly air bricks that you could see right through to a sparse open-ended lounge that ran the length of the house. I could even see the bare sandy garden on the other side and the thin blue threat of the ocean beyond. The ground floor seemed designed as a flow-through. A smart move that showed we do learn.

After a while, the woman came to the front door and beckoned. 'Come, inside. Tea is ready.'

She led me to a little yellow bench on the far side of the room. A small tea-table had been propped up in front of it with a piece of folded newspaper under one of the legs. Next to it an even more wonky stool. I took the bench.

'He is with our nona upstairs,' the housekeeper said. 'He said he will want you to take him to Colombo when he has finished here.' She lifted the little cosy she had put over the teacup and frowned.

'I can't just wait doing nothing,' I said.

'He won't be long. You had better wait. He comes every month but there's not much he can do with her. She won't move from her room. She just puts the AC full and stays inside.'

'Can't he call for a helicopter or seaplane or something? Isn't he a big shot?'

She smothered another heartless laugh. 'He must like you. You are a big joker, no? You have been joking with him? Most people are too frightened, you know, because you never know, no?' She drew her finger across her knotted throat with a big scary grin.

Then she left me to my cup of tea and went upstairs. I wondered what she meant. What would an officer like him do if he didn't feel like laughing at a joke? This is a lawful democratic republic, not some gangland playground. But then, I have to admit, sometimes it does feel like things have gone a bit funny lately. You don't expect to find a roving brigadier with no bodyguard, not even a gun, just a watch as big as the moon, buggered on the side of a road. Or a hostess in hiding, sealed in an air-conditioned room by the sea waiting for his honour. These days, it seems, anything could happen.

The saucer had a teaspoon with a tiny ceramic devil-mask clipped to the end. I held it by the ears and stirred my tea.

While I was trying to work out my options, the front door opened and a young man with a bandana around his head hopped in. He was dressed in welted denim and had crutches and only one leg. He pointed one of the crutches at me. 'Is that your van out there?'

I nodded.

'Put it to the side, machang. We have a party coming later.'

'I'll be gone soon,' I said.

'You just brought our army megastar, no?'

'Yes.'

'You'll be here for a while then. So, move it.'

He seemed too offhand to be running the guest house, but he had a half-cocked swagger that I didn't want to challenge. Although he was missing a leg, he looked like he was spoiling for a fight. His arms were big and muscly. He was the kind of soldier-in-disguise you find these days who was also near the top of my not-to-argue-with list.

I went out and moved the van. When I came back in, he was seated on the bench looking a bit calmer.

'So, is he here for like a regular party?' I asked, trying to be friendly.

'He's here to see my mother.' He nudged the stool my way with his crutch. 'Sit down. Make yourself comfortable. To repair a mistake takes time, even in the army. You have to go back over it again and again. You understand what I am saying?'

I can understand that a man, even a military man, might prefer the Versace-laced electric funk of a top-notch nightclub to the stink of soldiering in a swamp, but this guest house seemed neither here nor there.

'Is your mother the Manel of the guest house, or your father?'

'Not them.' He pulled out a cigarette from his blue shirt pocket and started chewing the end.

'It's not you, is it?'

'Why not?'

I thought soldiers were trained not to ask questions. Certainly not to answer back. That was the reason half the population of youngsters in these districts were being recruited into the army, wasn't it? A neat idea for a smooth social system. Or so I figured.

He lit his cigarette and his eyes clouded over. 'It is my name,' he said, 'but this is my mother's guest house.'

'I didn't think you were a hotelier,' I said. 'You must be a soldier, no?'

He patted the stump that had been his knee. 'What? Because of this?'

'Where'd you lose it?' I asked as if he'd misplaced his wallet, or I'd lost my marbles.

'Ask the big man. He can tell you.' He lit his cigarette and took a couple of rapid puffs. 'You think it's true that you can lose your legs smoking this stuff?' Then he pinched the cigarette out of his mouth and plunged it into my cup of tea.

I didn't want any more tea anyway. So I shrugged. 'I don't know.'

'I lost my brother too, in the same hellhole.' He let out a last lingering trace of smoke. 'They told our parents that we were both dead. Stupid donkeys. My father . . .'

'The brigadier?' For a moment I did wonder if he might be the father.

'He wasn't a brigadier then.' The crutch rose again in his hand and he pointed it towards the sea like some old cannon from the days of the Dutch. 'My father killed himself last year because he thought he'd lost both of us. My mother is slowly going nuts.'

I like to be able to make sense of the world around me.

That is what makes me comfortable. At this moment in history, in this country, perhaps that is a vain hope, but I like to think that if I had been in Moscow at the time of the Russian Revolution, or even in the Gulags of Stalin, I would have had a way, like my father with his ideology, of understanding how it all fitted together. I might have been wrong, and my logic badly mistaken, but it would have made sense to me, for the moment. I don't have to be right; I just want to be not confused. I am beginning to appreciate that it is a lot to ask for in this world, unless you are a firm religionist, but surely it is not too much?

'Is it his fault?' I asked.

Manel's shoulders dropped as though I had inadvertently released a catch. He looked lost. 'You can't tell who will walk in through that door and just wreck your life. You really can't.'

★

The footsteps coming down the stairs were heavy and deliberate. There was more than weight on the tread, or at least more than the weight of a living body. There was the weight we mean when we talk of things that weigh on your mind. It was a mind that was coming down the stairs. A mind in big black boots. The dancer in him, I guess, wore different shoes.

'Driver,' he said when he saw me, 'you are a lucky man.'

'Yes, sir,' I said. I was no longer the captain of a van. He was no longer a stray pickup.

'You can take me to Colombo now. You can go home after that.'

'That is good, sir.'

'You live in Colombo?'

'That side,' I said cagily, but he wasn't really listening. He was looking at Manel.

'I hear you got the job.'

Manel put a finger to his ear as if he was blowing his brains out. He wiggled it about. 'Fish. They want me to count fish for some Teheran company.'

'Prawns,' the brigadier corrected him. 'Crates of tiger prawns.'

'Right. Tiger fucking prawns. Remember the last time you talked to me about fucking tigers. You didn't know what the fuck you were talking about, did you?'

'You are lucky to get any job, if that's the way you talk.'

'Lucky to lose a leg as well I suppose.' He wiped his finger on his pointless knee.

'You got your compensation. Get over it, boy. Move on. Do your job and look after your mother now.'

Manel pulled in his lips, but couldn't stop the words

from bursting out. 'I'd like to see you move on, you know. Move on with one fucking leg.'

★

Fish, prawns, tigers are not my business. I carry people. On average about seventy kilos each, given that Mrs Klein in particular compensates for the likes of Vince, Paul and Miss Susila. What they carry on their consciences, in their hearts, guilt or grievance, is not for me to judge. I might sometimes help them unburden, but that is only partly out of curiosity. It is also my service. Same as the barber or the dentist, although with the razor and the drill, they have an advantage that tends to keep their mouths more open than their customers'—talking, I mean. I do it to aerate the van. Keep it bubbling. As far as I am concerned, what we talk about on the road is what we feel deep inside. You don't get that deep if you just sit still, whatever the yogis, the barbers and the dentists say. You need the sense of motion, your body hurtling through space. Then your thoughts can really move in your head. And if the conversation doesn't go beyond the parking situation at Odel's or the price of onions at Food City, well, then that's just the way you are. It is not that you are trivial, but only that that's the life you lead.

With the brigadier the possibilities were mind-boggling. I couldn't predict what would happen. We had a good 47 K to go. If he opened his mouth on this leg, he could spout blood, guts, terror or Tandoori Nights at the Little Hut. It was all there in him, waiting for the right trigger.

We stepped outside and he nodded at the old woman who had reappeared. 'Right,' he said. 'I'll go then and come back.'

She cringed and looked up at the window above us. I glanced up too and saw a lady all glammed up behind the glass.

Then the brigadier got inside the van and carefully sat in a different place from where he had been on the way to the guest house. Manel didn't come out.

'We'll go now?' I asked.

'Yes. Go, go,' he said with a hint of some loosish dance-floor rhythm bouncing in his blood.

I backed out of the gate. With an officer like him in my van, what was there to worry about on the road?

Once we were under way, I turned the AC down and tried to keep the engine noise steady. This was a man who could control a six-point spin of a dancing queen with one hand while decimating the most ruthless guerrilla force in the world with the other. I had to let him choose his own pace to speak, and hope for an improvement from the earlier journey. At least I knew that he was not averse to me and my style.

I was right.

'Driver, you think that boy is missing a screw or something?'

'Not mad, sir. Angry, maybe.'

'It happens with these fellows. Killing men from a war room is not a problem, but when you see them twitch, you know, it is another matter. If you see the face, Tiger or not. Or the body burst when you have pulled the trigger, then your life moves into a different sphere . . .'

'I think he is upset about himself, sir. His leg is the problem.'

'He has another.'

'Also his brother. No other brother. And no father, he said.'

'The whole family is fucked.'

'Sir?' I didn't know what to make of that, so I pressed the accelerator a bit more. My van sometimes flies like a bird. 'Which family, sir?'

'I have a plan,' he said. 'I have a plan for fellows like that. They need to be doing something routine, you know. You need a job, otherwise you get disaffected. A disaffected soldier, ex or not, is bad news. Especially if he is hooked to the killing side of things. You see, driver, it can be like a drug. You like a bit of speed, don't you?'

'Sir?'

'Foot on the pedal? A little lift? Well, you've never fired a gun, driver, have you?'

'No, sir. I was only a clerk before.'

'A bit of recklessness can be very tempting.'

'When you are driving for a living like me, sir, you cannot give in to recklessness. It is not good for business.'

'Driver,' he leant forward and tapped me on the shoulder. 'You are a very funny man. I like that.'

I tried to work out what was going on in his mind. 'Big officers are not reckless, are they?'

'Depends on the result. If things go right, you are seen as smart; if they go wrong, then you are called reckless.'

'But you, sir, you are the tops.'

'It also depends on who is looking at the result and where they stand.'

'Is that the problem with the boy?' I bit my tongue, too late. Drivers should drive and listen, not shoot off their mouth.

I felt the weight shift in the van. I checked the mirror and saw him smooth his hair. 'The boy is stuck in the past. You can't always be looking back. You have to look forward, no? Isn't that so, driver?'

'Yes, sir. You have to keep your eyes on the road.'

'Good. I am glad you understand that. This country needs people like you.'

When we first heard the war was over, we believed a line could be drawn between the mistakes of the past and the promise of the future. One was the place you had been, the other was the place you were going to. We believed there was no need for the two to be connected. But as a driver, I should have known better. To go from one to the other, you need a road. And a road is nothing if it doesn't connect. A bit like a knee. Bling or not, the brigadier knew that too.

Humbug

'Would you like one, Vasantha?' Miss Susila offered me a bag from behind. 'Sweets from England.'

'Thank you,' I said, keeping my eyes on the road. I picked something hard and popped it in my mouth. It was the most peculiar taste I had ever come across.

'I really like them, but not everyone does. Humbugs. Do you, Vasantha?'

It was difficult to reply. I managed a grunt of appreciation without choking. The peppermint certainly woke me up.

Miss Susila was too young and lovely to call 'madam'

even though she was married. She handed the bag of sweets to her husband and he put it in a plastic reseal sleeve and pinched the ridges at the edge together. It took him a couple of goes to get the grooves to fit. When it was done, he handed it back to her. It looked to me like the ritual of a much older couple.

'How much further to the rest house?' she asked.

'About twenty minutes,' I said. 'We will be there for lunch, no problem.'

'I'm starving,' she said.

'A long cool beer would do me very nicely,' her husband, Colin, added. He was an Englishman of the long kind. Everything about him was long: long legs, long body, long face, long nose. It was as though he had been modelled by a cartoonist long ago. But he had a very gentle manner and seemed to treat his wife with deference.

The road to Hambantota is very good. The best in the country now. The surface is first-class. It was not always so. There was a time when it was part of the wild country. But then it found political favour. Flavour of the month, year, decade, perhaps century. Now the talk is of highways, ports and airports, but all that is new. Ten years ago, people knew of the nicely situated rest house but not much more. It was the place to stop before you reached Yala and started looking for wild elephants and leopards.

'I can't believe we will *be* there,' Miss Susila said. 'For the last two years, I have been reading those pages over and over again.'

'Well, now you will see what it is really like.' Her husband's long pale fingers closed over hers briefly.

'It won't be the same. Gihan was saying that nothing much had changed for a hundred years, but then, in the last two or three, everything has changed. It is now the hub.'

'The sea must be the same.'

'That's what I really want. To hear the sea like Woolf did. I love that description he wrote about the surf dropping thud, thud on the beach.'

'The same sound every day, except the day the tsunami came.'

'I know. That's the thing.'

In my mirror I could see her bunch her hair at the back of her head and lift it off her neck and drop it. Her thoughts turning. Thudding.

I put the AC up a notch and took a bend in the road. The sea came leering into view, foaming in the blue bay. The couple in my van this time seemed about as unlikely a pair as you would ever find. Nothing matched except as opposites. Black and white, tall and short, calm and mad. She had a bag of books she wouldn't let go of, whereas he didn't even carry a pair of sunglasses. One liked speed, the rush of wind, the other preferred the languid air of a parked car. They were booked in for the night at one of the most expensive hotels, further down the coast, and yet wanted to lunch at the cheapest.

The challenge of my job is to fit these contradictions into one itinerary. A driver has to learn to do that. I haven't perfected the art yet but it is a lesson we could all do with, including the big honchos in their black Benzes.

★

The Hambantota Rest House was built on a promontory overlooking the bay. In the old days, when it stood alone, it would have been a very impressive building. A low but long, commanding, imperial presence. Now, despite overlooking the bay, the industriousness of the massive building works below it—dams, breakwaters, excavations—threatens to undermine its position. It has become marooned like a castaway on an island of its own.

I parked under the blossom trees and opened the door for Miss Susila.

'Thank you,' she said, breathing in the sea air. She jumped out, light as a feather.

Mr Colin unfolded for a minute or two before expanding to full size outside the van. 'Must have been a fabulous spot when Woolf was here.'

'The veranda on the other side is good for a cool drink,' I said. I had been here in 2002, before the tsunami, when the world of this coast was still half asleep from the previous century and before anyone dreamed that Hambantota might become the hub of the southern hemisphere. If she had come then, Miss Susila would have found the rest house just as she had imagined it from the books she had been reading of life in the jungle a hundred years ago. The bay was long and calm. The line of a wave that stretched for miles, rising and falling as regularly and as comfortingly as Mother Nature's breath. A few fishing boats sailing out, or sailing in. A sense that the growth of the interior had been brought to an abrupt close. At that time you wouldn't think there were more than a few hundred people dotted around the bay. I certainly could not have imagined 3000 there, and yet 3000 perished when the rogue tide came from the deep to take its toll. Ten times as many died up and down the coast. But now it is as if the town, the whole coastline, is dressing up for a party. I heard Mr Colin say something about the resilience of the people here. I suppose we must be resilient given all the things that have happened. Or else, it is a kind of scary collective amnesia.

'Come and join us,' Mr Colin said to me.

I followed them into the building.

It hadn't changed since the last time I had come. The same faded armchairs, a long, dark, dusty floor and greying white walls, a few bare tables. All slightly scruffy as one would have at home for want of money. Even the welcome flowers in the vase might have been the same ones dried out from ten years ago.

'I imagine in Woolf's day, there'd be more polish about,' Mr Colin said, looking around.

'The place would have been gleaming. He would have been a stickler for that kind of thing.' She gave her husband a telling look.

We walked through a jaded empty dining room to a back veranda that was smaller than I remembered. The long rattan chairs, yellowing and sagging in the middle, really could have been a hundred years old.

Miss Susila was in a dream, turning slow circles as she walked. Her husband followed watching her, and watching out for her, as though she was a child at play. Indulging her but at the ready to reach out if she strayed too close to the cliff, or came close to any danger.

'Please, sit down,' I said. 'I will go and find someone for you.' It was my duty as the only insomniac in the land of nod.

I went back into the main building. It was very odd that no one had appeared. I looked in the office but there was nobody there. Then I found a handbell that belonged to a ship or something. It looked like the sort of thing you might ring to warn of danger. Storms. Breaching whales. Madmen. Rather than swing it—I would have needed both hands to lift it—I tapped it on the side with my keys. There was no answer.

I went back to my tourists and found that they had had more success without me.

'This man is the only one here, Vasantha,' Miss Susila said to me. 'He says the place is closed.'

The young man standing next to her looked at me. He was dressed up in a tie and shiny black shoes; his hair was slick and spiky.

'Did your head office not tell you we are closed for refurb?'

I winced. 'No office, sir. I do private hire. I checked the website.'

'Tcha,' he clicked his tongue and frowned as though I was a fly-by-night cowboy taking advantage of a glitch in cyberspace to prey on innocents from abroad and therefore should be squashed as a matter of civic duty. He turned back to the others. 'I am very sorry. But if you come back next month, everything will be top class. Hot buffet, à la carte, acupuncture clinic, WiFi. Everything.'

'What about the building?' Mr Colin asked.

'Sir? Building the port is a big project. Phase 1, phase 2, phase 3. That will take more than one month more, but everything is on schedule.'

'I mean this building.'

'Oh, you mean the rest house building. This, you know, is very old. So my company has come with some big plans to modernize. Also in phases. That is the method now. Phase 1 is to knock that part down and put state-of-the-art bedrooms: climate control, rain-showers, triple X adult TV, you know. Full works. Then phase 2 is to go up. Build up.' He beamed. 'Up and up. We will have it nice and modern. Phase 3, we don't even know yet.'

'You can't,' Miss Susila cried. 'This is a historic building.'

The young man looked puzzled. 'It is very old, madam. It is not fit for purpose any more. It belongs to the British times, no?'

'Leonard Woolf was here.'

'Yes, yes. I know. They have his picture framed in the office. Famous man, no? Those days. Author of *The Village in the Jungle*. We had to study that book in school. We know all about him.'

'He writes about this house. It is an important place.'

'But, madam, that is a novel. All made up.'

'He would have sat just there. Look, I have his diary.'

'But this is not his house. The AGA bungalow was down the road. He only visited here for a bit of this and that. Anyway, madam, he is not here any more, no?' He gestured towards the veranda. 'What to do? We need to modernize for tomorrow's visitors, not yesterday's tiffin-tuckers.'

Miss Susila went limp. She looked close to tears. 'Even the tsunami didn't destroy it.'

'Nothing will be destroyed, madam. In fact, there is a plan to commemorate him in a real village in the jungle. Good, no? The Great Love Village.'

'What?' Mr Colin raised his long eyebrows. An involuntary prayer ruffled his temple.

'Buddhist Foundation project.'

'Sounds like some leftover hippie thing.'

'No. No. Love is what we need. Not all you need. Tzu Chi people designed the village, not the Beatles. Very major project. Relocation point for the people who lost everything in the tsunami. So, everything we have to start again. What else to do? In this country, you have to pick yourself up. Otherwise you get forgotten, no?'

I noticed Miss Susila's fists were clenched tight now. Her arms were growing rigid as though she was trying to straighten up. She was struggling to control her voice. 'So, all this will go?'

'Not go, madam. Renovate. Beyond recognition and very much better. You will like it, I can guarantee. Mr Woolf would love it, if he came back.'

'He is not coming back. He is dead.'

'I know. I know. But we will have ships down in the new harbour, and planes landing, one after another like in Heathrow, at the airport over that side. We will have visitors from all over the world. Real tourists. Indian, Chinese, Arab. And they will come back again and again, if we have the right standard, no? Not some olden-day thing.'

Miss Susila gasped, and then wordlessly turned away. Her shoulders were bunched, her tight denims drawn even tighter around her slim hips. She started towards the edge of the garden. The cliff drop.

Mr Colin took out a handkerchief and shook it. 'Can we get a cool drink and a sandwich at least?'

'Chicken sandwich? With tomato and mayonnaise?' The young man smiled, eager as ever.

'Yes, chicken would be good. No mayonnaise. Can you bring it soon?'

The smile froze. 'No, sir. Sorry, I cannot get you chicken, or anything for that matter. Not soon, not even tomorrow. The kitchen is closed. Cookie has gone to Kataragama for the refurb. No staff now. Nothing to do, no? I am only here for a catch-up with the manager but he called to say he had a puncture on the way.' He turned to me. 'Where are you taking them for tonight? What hotel?'

'We go to Tangalle,' I said.

'So, then no problem. You take them to the Hilltop Café for a bite. It's on the way. They can provide a good lunch. Even sandwiches, chicken or cheese. I think madam is hungry, no?' He smiled comfortingly.

Mr Colin had gone to her and was holding her shoulders. She shook in his arms, and sniffed. He found a tissue in his pocket and gave it to her.

'She was very excited about coming here,' I said to the manager. 'Talking all the time about that book.'

'Why look in some old book when you can see the future happening right here, before your eyes?' He leant forward, more like a conspirator than a hotel manager. 'Nona tikak pissu, neda?'

I was taken aback. He shouldn't talk like that about any visitor. We are a hospitable people. She wasn't mad. She was just upset about the change. I told him, he was the one who was off the rails. Stupid of me, as no doubt the future will bring me face-to-face with him again in some other tourist stop, and he, like all small-minded gaffers, would be offended and hold the grudge until his hand bled. But I couldn't let him get away with talking like that. 'No, sir. You are the one mixed up. Looking ahead but gear in reverse.'

Mr Colin called out to me. 'I think we better go, Vasantha.'

★

The Hilltop Café was situated at a bit of a height but in no way was it in as dramatic a position as the rest house. To call that bump on the road a hill was an exaggeration that even a politician would not resort to. There might have been a view of the sea once, but that was now obscured by a mound of earth from the excavations in the port. Luckily, the slope behind the open shed, dotted with the dark leaves of overgrown low-country tea bushes, gave some pastoral relief. Here and there fingers of encroaching jungle curled in, studded with violet flowers.

Miss Susila was still upset and so, while Mr Colin tended to her, I organized some mutton rolls and cheese pastries for them.

'Some black coffee, please,' Mr Colin called out. 'She needs some black coffee. That's the main thing.'

They sat opposite each other and waited with their arms straight out on the table like splints and holding each other's hands as if to steady themselves against another tide of misfortune. Together perhaps there is a chance. But what can you do alone?

While I was adding the coffee to the order, a man of very mature years came out of the back and shuffled slowly towards them. He had a large mellow face and a silvery semi-retired dome of a head. His nose and his lips looked eager as though they were features that had bloomed later than the frailer frame of his body. He stopped at the table, slightly stooped, swaying in the silent slow air discoloured by the ceiling fan. Then he cleared his throat and asked Mr Colin, 'Are you from England?'

'Yes,' Mr Colin conceded, sharp and uncharacteristically short, clearly not in the mood for more local interaction.

'Where in England?'

'London,' Mr Colin snapped.

'Very good.' The old man breathed a sigh of relief. He moved his head forward and tilted it up, like some prehistoric bird hoping to take flight. He picked a newspaper clipping out of his breast pocket and slowly unfolded it. He smoothed it out on the table. 'I think, sir, you can help me then.'

'I don't think so,' Mr Colin said, trying hard to be curt but not impolite. He knew how to keep his purse closed.

The old man looked at him as though he was a child. 'But you don't know what I am asking.'

'I know.'

'My name is Abeysinghe. Rex Abeysinghe. I have never been to London.'

Mr Colin could not be completely uncivil. 'Colin Stonebrook.'

'From London north? Or south?'

'North.'

'Excellent. Then you are indeed the person I very much need.' Mr Abeysinghe smiled absently to himself. 'You see, the problem I have is the Northern Line.'

Mr Colin was caught off guard. He looked at him in surprise. Hooked. 'What?'

'The clue, four across, is "concerns men rotting differently under GMT star always after Islamic breakfast". Two words, ten and eight ending with T. But what is an Islamic breakfast in London today?'

'How do you get Northern Line?' Mr Colin asked, with a quietening glance at his wife.

'GMT must be a line in London. Under the star therefore is the Northern Line underground, no?'

Mr Colin tipped his head to one side. 'May I see?'

Mr Abeysinghe pushed the clipping across. 'I thought the train to Paris, with that business of the veil in France, might have a connection, but the T is in the wrong place. No chance for Eurostar. Or the move from Waterloo to St Pancras.'

Mr Colin studied the clipping. 'This is from a British paper?'

'My cousin sends me a batch every month. He collects them and posts them. The solution to this one will come next week.'

Miss Susila had withdrawn into a shell, her hands hidden under the table, but her husband, clearly intrigued, toyed with a butter knife. Suddenly, his face lit up. 'Station to station. Yes. You are right to go continental but it is not croissant. The second word "after" must be a crescent.'

'The anagram then is in the first three words, not two?'

'Exactly.' Mr Colin tapped the table with the butt of the knife. 'Mornington Crescent.'

The old man was delighted. 'Oh, I say. Very good, sir. Very good. That, I believe, is the station that is always the answer, is it not?' He licked the sharpened end of his pencil and filled in the line of blank boxes. 'The moment I saw your face, I knew I should ask you.'

'Glad I could help. Islamic, huh. That's sailing close to the edge, isn't it? Turkish might have been safer but I suppose any place can blow up now. Which paper is it?'

'I can tell the setter, but not the paper. My cousin cuts it to the minimum, so I have never known. Airmail, you know. Every gram is critical, given the price of stamps nowadays.' He showed a tiny space between finger and thumb where a penny might drop. 'In any case I'd rather not know which oligarch I need to thank for my mental stimulation. But tell me, sir, what brings you to these parts? So far from Mornington Crescent?'

'My wife has an interest in this area.'

Mr Abeysinghe turned to her, panting at the exertion. 'Family, madam? Political?'

'No,' she stiffened another notch in her spine, clearly unwilling to be drawn into a pointless conversation.

Mr Colin, however, seemed to have found something to connect with in the old man. 'Woolf,' he said. 'We are interested in Leonard Woolf. You know of him, no doubt.'

Mr Abeysinghe put away his pencil and puzzle. A smile widened like a wave across his face. 'This time, I can be the one who helps you, Mr Stonebrook. I know all about Leonard Woolf. I even met him when he came back to Ceylon in 1960.'

Miss Susila stared at him in disbelief. A fly flew past her and she didn't even notice. 'No.'

'It is true, madam. No humbug. I met him and we spoke for a long time that afternoon. You see, my father had worked in the katcheri with him here in Hambantota, back in 1908, when Mr Woolf came as Assistant Government Agent. On promotion from Jaffna, I believe, or perhaps Kandy. At any rate, Mr Woolf remembered him, you know. A fine memory and a fine gentleman. He wanted to know about my father. Sadly, although my father learnt a great deal from Mr Woolf, he did not learn the secret of a long life. He passed away in 1952. But he was very fond of Mr Woolf. He admired him greatly.'

'He spoke about Leonard Woolf?'

'Oh, yes, madam. He was determined to pass on the wisdom of Mr Woolf to me. It had a most profound effect. His book, which my father directed me to, again and again, gave me my love of literature. From the village in the jungle to the lighthouse, you might say. And his training gave me my profession. I became an accountant.'

Both Mr Colin and Miss Susila were spellbound. 'Was your father certified?' Mr Colin asked.

'No, sir. He was a clerk. Very reliable. In those early years of administration, Mr Woolf had a highly developed sense of economy and of public service. Two things he impressed upon my father. One was the requirement to respond to the ordinary man's need for justice immediately. Any inquiry at the Assistant Government Agent's office, any problem raised, had to be responded to on the day itself. "No pending tray, was his motto," my father used to say. No waiting for tomorrow. It is a lesson our modern bureaucracy has completely forgotten.'

'Unfortunately, that is very true all over the world,' Mr Colin said. 'Especially in England these days.'

'The second, and this I now believe I misunderstood in my youth, and to my cost. Or perhaps I understood it but only at the lowest level of interpretation, rather than at its most profound.'

A waiter brought the plate of deep-fried rolls, patties, and crisp cheese straws that I had ordered and placed them in the centre of the table. 'Tomato ketchup, sir?' he asked Mr Colin.

'Yes, yes,' he replied quickly to pack him off.

'I am sorry,' Mr Abeysinghe said, taking a step back. 'I am interrupting your lunch. Forgive me. At my age, my enthusiasms often outstrip my manners.'

'No, no. Please sit down. Join us. Have a mutton roll?'

'Do go on.' Miss Susila was doe-eyed.

'The second?' Mr Colin asked. 'What was the second lesson?'

'Well, to finish the point, one must understand Mr Woolf was very meticulous with the details of daily life. My father said he had the admirable habit of noting down every recordable fact, you understand? From the number of limes on the lime bush in his garden to the cost of every provision in the household. Not just sugar and flour, but every onion and puppadom. I don't know how his wife, Virginia, managed with him in bohemian Bloomsbury. He was most particular about expenditure and income and documented everything. Not a cent would go unaccounted in his house here. And therefore you can imagine how scrupulously he maintained the records of tax and revenue. Private money should not be wasted unwittingly, he would say, but public money should not be misused unwittingly, or wittingly.'

I edged in a bit closer. I was beginning to warm to this mysterious English Woolf-man. There were lessons here for us all, but Mr Colin did not seem to really get it.

'You say you misunderstood? What do you mean?' he asked.

Mr Abeysinghe turned out his hands as though he was chucking notes in the air. 'I thought an accountant would do justice to those principles, but you see at that level you are only adjusting columns in a ledger.'

'Is that not fundamental?'

'Perhaps. But you know, these days numbers have become complete fictions. How do you write a trillion in a double-entry ledger and still make it meaningful in a world where an ordinary man must do with less than ten dollars a day? Even Mr Woolf would find it difficult not to let his mind wander.'

'Have a pattie, at least?' Mr Colin nudged the plate.

'Thank you, but I have intruded far too long. I shall be on my way. But I wonder, sir, madam—Might I ask you one more favour? Might you have some books you would be willing to part with before you go? You see,

I have started a little library here. I am an accountant with a library. A community library. I try to collect any books that visitors might have finished with and wish to leave behind. Tourists often have better things to take back than the books that they brought to read by the pool. Unless they have gone electronic and consume their reading in the new tablet form, they need to divest themselves and we can help in that. It would be nice to find what Mr Woolf would call literature or history, but we need books, no matter what. Self-help, Crime, Thrillers.'

Mr Colin looked at his wife. 'Perhaps the Woolf books would be ideal?'

'What? Crime?' She started.

'Your books, madam? If you are finished with them, maybe you can donate?'

'My books? These?' She pulled her London book-bag close.

Mr Abeysinghe's mouth flapped like a dog's. 'I am by necessity having a very eclectic collection. Last month, it was the most extraordinary female erotica from Australia. But everything has a place, in my view.'

'Impossible. I cannot leave these.'

Her husband pursed his lips thoughtfully. 'It might be a very appropriate gesture given the heritage. We can get them replaced, my dear, when we get back.'

'No.' She zipped up her bag. 'No. These are mine. You can send some others, Colin, when we go back home.'

'Home?' Mr Colin stopped himself from saying something else.

The old man raised a hand in surrender. 'I understand, madam. One must keep one's favourites close. No matter. Nobody reads here anyway. The whole idea of mine is foolish and ridiculous. What they will be wanting in this town is coffee and tarts. Not books, especially not ones that might tell us of what might have been. The culture we revel in now is the culture of impunity.'

'We will send you some books from London.' Mr Colin pulled out a smartphone. 'Give me your address.'

'No, sir. Shipping these days is a waste of money. Even to send a crossword from England costs more than a lunch packet here. I can see that from the postage my cousin pays. I feel guilty enough as it is every month. I try to keep an account, but I know I will never be able to repay him. Forget the books, sir. They are only words, after all. My foolish fantasy. Castles in the air. Isn't that what they say? We have more serious things to occupy us. We have the whole world going mad to contend with here. If anyone does want to read, well, they can write something themselves, can't they?'

He might have been joking, but Mr Colin was upset. He didn't seem to know what to do.

'In that case, how about a sweetie for now?' Mr Colin looked pleadingly at his wife.

I kept my mouth shut. You can make up the future, but I am not sure you can do that with the past and still be yourself.

Miss Susila was still flushed and tense but she pulled out the packet of hard-boiled sweets from her bag and handed it over to Mr Abeysinghe. 'Would you like one of these?' she asked. 'They are from England.'

Running on Empty

Some nights, I just want to drive. We can do that now. No curfew, no roadblocks. Only a toll plaza, and that's a long way off out of town. The cost of petrol is high, but if I need to be in the van on my own, carrying no one, going nowhere, remembering nothing, loafing, I can do it. I tap in the cassette Mrs Cooray left in the van and turn up the volume, pretending the bouncy song is about me: *Mister Van Man, bring me a dream* . . . I swing down to Narahenpita, jiggling the wheel, go up Park Road, then right on to Havelock and a sharp left into Dickman's rib. When I reach Galle Road, in the dead of the night, I step on it and head for the Colombo Fort hoping that some magic will be caught in my beam.

This place becomes a secret city at night. It has always been like that. In the old days, when we had the war in the north that we never talked about, hardly anybody would be out after nine at night. No need for a curfew. The streets were dark. Only a few VIP cars cruised about, doing deals, or a solitary three-wheeler puttering home, having risked a night in hell for a last fare. Nobody on foot who didn't wear a uniform and a gun. That's all gone now, thankfully.

Now the streets are clean, hosed down. The decades-old debris of blown-up banks cleared, the burnt-out carcases of buses carted away. The oil barrels of makeshift checkpoints gone, mostly, and even the grey walls that hid all our minor fortresses have been demolished. There are coloured lasers instead, and salsa dance dens and traffic lights winking. If I turn at Colpetty, down past the old market where the destitutes try to hide, and take the roundabout by the cinema and head back on Duplication, even after midnight, I see party people tumbling out of blacked-out German cars into coffee bars and nightclubs—the few who have more money than sense. The ones who are forever carefree, who have never cared about anything but themselves. Perhaps they know something the rest of us don't and are enjoying whatever they can get hold of before the coffers run dry. Sometimes it feels like this is now a country of no consequences. But then, someone gets shot for speaking out of turn, or saying the wrong thing, and you realize that there are consequences after all.

So, what to do? Follow the swing, not the ball, as my father used to say, and step on the gas?

I go straight past the beautiful presidential Temple Trees, the last of the camouflage sentries and dun-coloured sandbags still guarding the residence, right up to Galle Face where the old hotel is lit up. This Christmas they had more fairy lights than an elephant on parade and the biggest tree outside the entrance since the crazy days of the 1950s. I remember coming as a boy with my father to see those fancy decorations. Or was it to polish the golf clubs of some visiting champion staying there? Maybe the one with the peachy turban who was a big hit at the ladies' tea. A real sandman bringing a dream. The hotel is over a hundred years old. It has seen the best and the worst of times. Days of plenty, days of strife. Japanese Zeros heralding the Second World War, Sunday crowds eating pink candyfloss, army parades turning the grass to dust, athletes in training, magicians and charlatans of every shade, kite flyers, Tiger moths, suicide bombers, wedding couples on the cusp. They come and are briefly illuminated, then all too quickly completely forgotten in the noontide's toll.

We now have palm trees planted along the road. The military camp on the other side has gone and another hotel is due to be built. Someone said it might be Chinese. The newest opposite the oldest. Ahead, the darkness of night is being burnt off by the bright lights of the port where container ships are coming in from Hong Kong and places I have never heard of. The skyline is rising. I like to drive right down to the end past the Beira, where the water is dark and the pelicans sleep, and take a turn in front of the old stone parliament building, so small and insignificant beside the five-star concrete monsters that have grown around it. No one stops me. I check my rear-view mirror.

Occasionally around here, some low-slung Porsche burns rubber for a second or two and shoots in front of me up towards the Hilton and the new chic plaza of the renovated Dutch Hospital: a flash of a girl with bare arms and sparkling teeth, a burst of exhaust like gunfire. It will be a Lamborghini soon enough, the way things are going. I step right down on the accelerator, wanting to feel a Samurai surge too, as if this was another night race, but the old Toyota can't go very fast. It has taken me all the way from the northern tips of Jaffna's wounded streets down to the flooded coves on the south coast, beyond

Mirissa, and every mile is logged in my mind but it feels like we have all been spinning in sand. I carry a big load now, wherever I go, from the yearnings of teenagers to the heartache of soldiers. I carry more than dreams. There is so much in my head I wonder how I will ever get it out. How do I do it before it is too late? Before I forget what has happened, what I saw, what I thought, what I believed on all those journeys north and south. The hopes, the aspirations, the secret guilt embedded in our shaken lives. Before I give up on the stories that make us who we are and drift with the tide into oblivion like every other sleepy grey head in the world.

I turn left and head for Union Place where, in a fit of madness, I can spend a day's hire on a masala pizza at my favourite neon joint. I park my van right outside the big glass door. There are no dossers on the pavement, no queues at the counter. My luck is in.

'Extra topping on your pizza, Mister Van Man?' Nisha, in her funny hat, sings.

'Yes,' I reply. 'Yes. Put a couple of extra green chillies, please, and can I have a cold beer on the side?'

She sprinkles stardust in a circle like a healer and smiles as if tonight, as darkness falls, she might just bring me everything.

Acknowledgements

My thanks to Sigrid Rausing and Chiki Sarkar for their enthusiasm, and their teams at Granta and Penguin India for running full speed with this book. Thanks to Bill Hamilton for finding a road map and special thanks to Curtis Gillespie for a crucial gear change, early in the day, Helen and Shanthi for fine-tuning, Tanisa for the flag, and Nanyang Technological University for a refuelling stop on the last lap. Thanks also to the many friends met on the road, north and south, and especially behind the wheel in Sri Lanka whose stories led me to Vasantha's van.

Also by Romesh Gunesekera and available from Granta Books
www.grantabooks.com

REEF

Shortlisted for the Booker Prize 1994

'A sensuous feast of delight, incessantly pleasurable to read' *The Times*

Reef is a love story set in the disintegrating paradise of Sri Lanka.
It is told by Triton, who at the age of eleven goes to work as houseboy to
Mister Salgado, a marine biologist obsessed by swamps, sea movements
and the island's disappearing reef. Triton learns to polish silver; to mix
a love cake with ten eggs, creamed butter and fresh cashew nuts; and to
steam the exotic parrot fish for his master's lover. As Triton recounts his
story, an extraordinary voice emerges: naive and knowing, fearful and
brave, a boy becoming a man in a world on the brink of chaos.

'Dark as one of Graham Greene's tropical undergrowths, funny in the way
that Naipaul can be, multi-layered in the manner of Joyce, evocative as
Narayan, *Reef* is a thing of beauty' *Scotland on Sunday*

'A kind of Asian *Tempest*, drenched in the unreal
tropical colours of dream' *Guardian*

'A book of the deepest human interest and moral poise . . .
Very few contemporary novels combine at so high but natural a pitch
qualities of epic strength and luminous intimacy' *Independent on Sunday*

Also by Romesh Gunesekera and available from Granta Books
www.grantabooks.com

MONKFISH MOON

A *New York Times* Notable Book

'These sad, spare stories illustrate the shocking fragility
of the whole modern world' *New York Times*

Written with startling grace, these nine haunting stories create a
compelling picture of Sri Lanka, a country of teeming natural beauty
and a society in turmoil, where a sudden silence in a city brings fear,
and where one night a young girl goes dancing while on another
a man discovers his life is ending.

'Graceful and grim, [these stories] constitute carefully civilized bulletins
on barbarity's reverberations' *Sunday Times*

'Gunesekera's language has a simple surface – but the simplicity is
deceptive; his observation is as close as the stare of a voyeur' *Independent*

'Full of the uncertain sadness of exiles and dreamers . . . Gunesekera's
characters become memorable emblems of solitude and despair . . . [His]
prose pulses with precision, without stridency or showiness' *Vogue*

'The insistent beauty of Sri Lanka is in poignant contrast to the violence of
the times . . . The delicate firmness with which Gunesekera portrays
the dilemmas of living in a spoiled paradise gives his collection
a haunting, eye-opening quality' *Observer*

THE SANDGLASS

'Outstanding' Penelope Fitzgerald

Moving between London and Sri Lanka, *The Sandglass* tells the story of two feuding families whose lives are interlinked by the changing fortunes of postcolonial Sri Lanka. Sliding back and forth between two physical and temporal locales, the novel vividly brings to life Prins Ducal and his search for answers about his family's past, including his father's rise to wealth, rivalry with the Vatunas family and a suspicious death.

Weaving together themes of memory, exile and postcolonial upheaval, *The Sandglass* is an unforgettable novel.

'A novel of true distinction, the work of a profoundly honest mind' *Independent on Sunday*

'Behind the narrative's deft and subtle interweavings of elaborate histories and fugitive memories, crashed dreams and still moments of promise, there lie strong echoes of Thomas Hardy's poetry with its delicate images of remembered pleasures and visions of despoiling loss' *Times Literary Supplement*

'Elegiac, freighted with melancholy, *The Sandglass* paints a vivid portrait of a society in that recent past and in a frightening present' *Independent*

'A mature meditation on time and death. There is a desperate sadness to it, which is totally engrossing. It is a brave, beautiful novel, which confronts chaos with relaxed wit and elegance' *Sunday Telegraph*

Keep in touch with
Granta Books:

Visit grantabooks.com to discover more.

GRANTA